The
First
Honeymoon

New and Selected

Stories

By Lyn Coffin

First Iron Twine Press Edition, April 2015

Published by Iron Twine Press

Five of these stories first appeared in other publications: "A Gift Horse" was published in The Bridge; "Her Political Body" appeared in Rackham Review; "A Lesson In Black and White" appeared in Ball State Forum; "Falling Off the Scaffold" was first published at Michigan Quarterly Review and reprinted in Best American Short Stories, 1979 (Houghton Mifflin Harcourt publishers); "On the Topmost Branch of a Beckett Tree" was published online at Big Bridge (bigbridge.org)

Iron Twine Press ISBN: **978-0692318508**

Book Cover Design by Mariana Jasso

www.Irontwinepress.com

Lyn Coffin is an award-winning fiction writer, poet, playwright, and translator. Sixteen books of her writing have been published, and her plays have been presented internationally. Her short stories have appeared in magazines, journals and anthologies, including the *Best American Short Stories* edited by Joyce Carol Oates. She teaches literary fiction at the University of Washington. Lyn holds an honorary PhD from the World Academy of Arts and Culture (UNICEF) "for poetic excellence and her efforts on behalf of world peace."

For Leif

CONTENTS

THE
FIRST
HONEYMOON

NEW AND SELECTED STORIES

A GIFT HORSE

Denise was sure she was right to have said what she did, until Leah left for school. Then misgivings rushed upon her, waves cresting into cavalry horses, a soldier on every one.

The shop girl smiled again. What was she waiting for? Oh, yes. She was supposed to buy something. At least look at something. The counter and showcase were littered with china bric-a-brac. She had come seeking something for Leah—an angel, possibly. Leah needed something to take Santa's place. But porcelain figurines weren't right for a seven-year-old, even the most careful.

What could she have been thinking of?

Death. She'd been thinking of death. Her death. Her "impending" death. Only it was more as if death had been thinking of her. She hadn't had any medication this morning, wanting her thinking clearer. It was, too. But the pain in her gut had gone crazy.

"Leah," she began, "suppose you were grown-up and had a daughter and you loved the daughter very

3

much the way I love you and let's suppose your daughter believed something and the something made her happy but wasn't true. Would you tell your daughter the truth? Or would you let her go on believing in the thing that wasn't true but made her happy?"

The salesgirl wasn't smiling now. Denise flailed about in her mind, searching for what her mother had called "some saving grace." She looked at the girl's white plastic badge. "HELLO! My Name is Beth!" said the thick, aqua letters. Maybe some time in the 21st century, Leah would be a salesgirl here. No, the imagination was a round-eyed bank teller and truth produced a six-shooter and pulled the trigger. The truth was, she would never live to see her daughter grow up. Somewhere inside her, a tumor was growing like Topsy. A storm was brewing. It was time to batten down the hatches, only there were no more hatches left.

This young woman wanted to please her—no, more than that—she wanted to do right. The beautiful young always did. "I love you, mommy. Are you mad at me?" That was Leah these days, and they went over and over the truth as if it were a role that needed to be memorized. They went over and over what was coming until the future was a stone rolling downhill, away from the tomb. And every morning, there it was to deal with again. Surprise, surprise, surprise.

"Leah, sweetheart! I told you this nasty cancer thing isn't because of you."

"Who's it because of, then?"

Denise waited, afraid to answer too soon, before the dust of emotion had settled, and truth stood revealed. "It's not because of anyone, sweetie. Not you or me or daddy or anyone."

"I think it's God," Leah said. "I think he did this to you. Why are you looking like that? It's the truth. That's what I think!"

"But why? Am I so bad God has to gun me down?" And Leah looked down at her and there were honest to god tears brimming over her lower eyelids. "No, mommy. Not you. He's the one that's bad. When I get big I'm going to tell people not to vote for him."

Beth was leaning forward, peering at Denise with a mixture of sympathy and satisfaction, distaste and curiosity. Denise tried to look at her, but it was like looking at someone through smoke or water. The girl had big blue eyes, almost like Leah's. She had blonde brown hair which floated out from the sides of her face. There were spots of color in her cheek, too dramatic and uneven to be anything but natural. Her dark eyebrows had been plucked almost to extinction. Maybe Beth's mother had a thing about facial hair. Oh, but she, Denise, must try to be where she was, and not hidden somewhere inside it. She mustn't let death, the fact of it, drive her underground. Leah was counting on her, Richard too. And Beth—right here, right now—was leaning forward, waiting. Perhaps Beth was an angel in disguise.

Denise fished around inside herself and found her voice. She dragged it up to the surface. It was a magic fish with a ring in its mouth. What would it say?

"I'm sorry, Beth."

The words were right, but the tone was wrong—a preface to some important, difficult rite. Denise could see the young husband who would say those words. He would be in his study, late one mild winter's night. He would be smoking a pipe—No. Forget the pipe. But he would be pacing, unable to look at his shivering wife. "I'm sorry, Beth," he would say. "I don't know how to go on without you."

"Excuse me?" Beth said.

Denise focused on her with a start. Beth had the tonality down flat. When she said "Excuse me," the tone let you know she had nothing to be excused for. Maybe Beth was an angel, after all. Or maybe she was just young and pretty and underpaid.

"I'm a little spacey these days," Denise heard herself say. The words gave her courage: she picked up a blue china horse the size of a Kleenex box. When you were holding something, people didn't so strongly expect you to talk. No, that was wrong. You didn't so strongly need to talk. That must be it.

Denise held the horse up to Beth. It was garish and old-looking. Almost unbearably cheerful. "How much is this?"

Beth smiled again. When she smiled, she moved her head a little and her tiny globe earrings began to swing. Denise felt ice forming under her feet. She was on a playground, about to slide. The slide was so long, you couldn't see the end. There were boys down there with dogs. She focused on the end of Beth's nose. It was a nice nose, with a nice end. "Let's go powder our noses," her mother would say, when she needed to go to the bathroom.

"It's on sale for $49, ma'am," Beth said. "Part of our Christmas clearance."

Denise nodded..."Ma'am"..."Seems like kind of a lot," she said. The conversation was beginning to feel okay—a pair of jeans which had shrunk in the wash.

Beth seemed taken aback. "It was $69 before the clearance," she said somewhat primly. Denise wanted to take her hands and reassure her. "Never mind," she wanted to say. "Don't take it personally."

Beth reached across the counter and took the horse out of her hands. "Look," she said. "This is why." She turned the horse so it faced Denise and held it up at eye-level.

The horse's mouth was wide open, in the kind of exaggerated yawn usually associated with hippos. "I guess this particular gift horse—" Denise began.

Beth shook her head as if shaking off flies. "Look inside," she said.

Denise took her so-called reading glasses out of her pocket and put them on. The horse's mouth leapt into sudden focus.

And then she saw. The inside of the mouth and all down the throat, as far as the eye could travel—her eye at least—everything had been painted. The primary color was a Pepto-Bismol pink and not a

7

little jarring. But there were other colors too, and after another visual adjustment, Denise began to make out scenes. The inside of the horse was an unbroken continuum of tiny landscapes, punctuated with small houses, tiny trees, even, yes, dotted with infinitesimal people.

And Leah looked up at her with those eyes, those eyes which were not Richard and not Denise but Leah now, Leah only. "I'd tell her the truth, mommy," she said. And her lower lip trembled. And when Denise told her—"There isn't any Santa Claus, Leah. Not really."— she didn't make a sound, though tears slid silently down her cheeks, one after the other. She said nothing until she was almost out of the room. "Why didn't you tell me he wasn't really real before?" she said. "Why did you let me believe in Santa Claus all the way until now? Didn't you know?"

"Wow." Denise put the horse down. Her hands had become perpetually cold but sweaty. It was hard to hang on to anything.

Beth smiled. "Do you like it?" She asked, not without a trace of eagerness. The questions of the young were never without a trace of eagerness. It was like a badge for them.

"Well..." Denise paused. She had, as Richard would say, "a thing about honesty." She wouldn't lie, even out of kindness. In her opinion, lying was always a mistake. The truth was always what people needed to hear, even when the truth came like a frozen turkey, wrapped in blood-stained words like

"Four weeks to a year."

"It's fascinating," she said. "I'm not sure I really like it, though."

Beth nodded, but looked crestfallen. When she nodded, her badge bobbed up and down. Denise admired the way Beth had pinned it on, right at the very tip of her left breast, so it hung a little bit over and down into space. It reminded Denise of her mother's favorite story. A man of faith is dangling over a cliff, hanging on by one hand. He calls to God. God says, "If you believe in me, let go." The man responds, "Is there anyone else up there I could talk to?"

Beth's disappointment seemed to have modulated into something like sadness. Maybe she hadn't sold anything all morning. Maybe she worked on commission. Maybe her boyfriend made these horses. Maybe Beth too was actively dying. Maybe she wasn't real.

Denise looked around. They were trying a new medicine. It made her mouth dry. Richard was sitting by her bed. She asked him for water. He poured a glass and held it out to her. When she reached for the water, though, her hand closed on air. There was no glass of water there. Denise looked over at Richard, to complain, and he had vanished as well. Later they told her the medicine was a cousin to the stuff glue-sniffers sniffed. Hallucinations were one of many possible side-effects.

Leah stood in the doorway, waiting for an answer, a truthful answer. "Of course I knew Santa

Claus wasn't real, sweetie. I just didn't realize he was a lie before. Then when I saw what you wrote to him about the reindeer—"

Beth smiled shyly, about to confess a misdemeanor. "Look," she said. "I figured this out last night."

She took the horse in both hands and gently set it back down on its haunches. It looked absurd, but endearing: a horse impersonating a dog, sitting up and begging for biscuits. Pathetically eager to please.

Denise nodded, but it was like with the CAT and MRI scans—she didn't know what she was supposed to see. Once she had been at a dump. She looked around and saw nothing unusual for a dump until Richard pointed it out: on top of the smoldering heap someone had put an enormous dead boar, all pink and gray and gristle-greasy, a probable casualty of PCB. "You let your expectations tell you what to see, instead of the other way around," Richard said on the way home. Then he proposed, which really confused her. "I don't know what to say," she told him. "Do you love me?" he asked. "Oh, yes," she said, grateful that, for once, the truth was easy.

"Dear Santa"—the slanting, ropey letters struggled their way uphill and even off the page. "I hope your haveing a nicer Xmas than we are. My mommy says she is dieing and she always tells the truth. So what I want for Xmas is for her to stop. I hope you can arange this right away. Let me know if I can help. I'll leave a plate of coukies for you and your raindear under the tree. Yours Truely, Merry Xmas.

Love, Leah"

"I don't know where this came from, but I think it's really neat," Beth said. "They probably got it out of someone's tomb or something." Her voice sort of wriggled away at the end of the sentence and she did not look up. Maybe the store had seminars where guys in plaid sports jackets instructed salespeople on what not to mention. "Forget about death and taxes!" he would thunder. "Death and taxes are no-no's!"

Beth took off the old-fashioned double-strand pearl choker she was wearing and looked around nervously, as if afraid someone might see what she was doing, and disapprove.

Denise shook her head. She and Beth were the only ones at the counter. They were alone, for all practical purposes. The only significant sound—she did not count the interminable Muzak — "You better watch out, you better not cry"— was the high-pitched babble of children somewhere in the distance. Lining up for Santa, no doubt. Santa must have overslept. Probably had a hangover and no kids of his own.

Beth dangled the choker over the horse's mouth pendulum-fashion, and smiled as though she and Denise were friends. No, not friends—co-conspirators.

"Look." Beth let the choker sink into the horse, like a snake-charmer's snake, collapsing back onto itself. "See?" She smiled at Denise, confidently now, as if she had known Denise all her life. Denise tried

11

not to feel pleased, but couldn't quite manage it. "You can put valuables and stuff in it."

Beth sighed, upended the horse, and dumped the choker out into her hand. She didn't put it back around her neck, just stared at it as if she weren't sure whose it was, and shoved it into what was presumably her black handbag—a rabbit back into the hat.

"Thanks for showing me," Denise said. "But I've never really understood the appeal of that." Beth looked at her blankly. "You know, teapots shaped like elephants, pitchers shaped like pigs, so you pour your tea out of a long nose, or milk out of a pig's snout."

"I like things to be useful, though. Don't you?" Beth gazed wistfully down at the horse. When Denise looked like that at home, Richard came running with equipment, and a good thing, too. "I think I'm in the wrong department," Beth confided. "I'd quit but I only got the job last week. Besides, I need the money."

"Never mind," Denise told her. "I want to buy the horse. My daughter has a lot of jewelry. And she loves odd containers. You remind me of her, actually. She'll probably like it just fine. If she doesn't, I'll ask my husband to return it, that's all. He's an architect, but semi-retired, so he has time for stuff like that."

"Oh..." Beth's expression was glazed and guarded now. Probably afraid she, Denise, was about to launch into her life's story. An X-rated one at that.

"Do you want this gift-wrapped?" Beth asked. "It

costs a dollar extra."

"That's okay," Denise said.

"'That's okay', meaning 'yes', or 'That's okay', meaning 'no'?"

"I'll have it gift-wrapped," Denise told her. "Price is no object these days."

Beth smiled ruefully. "I wish I could say that."

Denise just nodded.

She took a cab home, then ruined the ride—the last trip by herself; she had promised Richard, the last trip *as* herself—by evaluating her performance most of the way. True, she had been her all too usual self again. She had not done much for Beth's day, or advanced her good opinion of humankind. But she hadn't thrown up or been insulting. She had bought something Leah would like. She had not mentioned anything to do with death or dying, even on cue.

She was shaking from the effort any sustained motion now required. She felt feverish, uncoordinated. Intoxicated. On the verge of losing it. She knew what Richard would say when he heard how her self-billed "final shopping spree" had gone. He would lecture her with his arms folded, all the while pacing and looking out the window. He would say, "Was some damn knick-knack really worth all this?" And she would tell him the truth. "Absolutely not."

He was an emotional accountant, which made sense from the "opposites attract" perspective. Denise's mother had once read in a woman's magazine that for each cigarette smoked one might have to deduct as much as an hour of life: she had spent all day figuring it out, and announced to Denise that, given her daily quota of nicotine, she had died four hours before her birth.

Richard would let the matter drop, in deference to the fact she was dying. He had always been like that, paying deference to facts. In her situation, he kept saying, he would have "paced" himself, taking long naps and mega-vitamins. He would have begun an intensive "research" campaign, trying to find out what was killing him before it did.

She didn't care about that. Her efforts, misguided as they obviously were, had been in another direction.

She turned the package on her lap. There was no doubt Leah would like the horse. For how long, though—that was the key question with Leah. Maybe it was the key question with everyone. Leah liked everything she got, which was part of being seven, and greedy. She was greedy for gifts, greedy for attention, greedy for truth. But satisfaction paled quickly.

She began to think about tombstones again. Leah had come up with a good one. "Loving Mother and Wife of Three." Denise had told Leah the truth about her former husbands, the truth about her cancer, the truth about her dying. Richard said she was being morbid and "over-taxing" Leah's imagination.

Never mind, Denise told herself. Telling the truth is who you are, and what you do best. She had

Richard's love but, truthfully, she would have liked his approval as well.

She had worked in a hospice right up until the time of her own diagnosis. Then she quit. Quit before they could ask her to leave. Quit before anyone could uncover and wrest from her the one great, guilty secret. She was afraid—No, she was *terrified* of dying.

Not of the pain. She had a lifetime of experience in dealing with pain. She was an expert. Not of embarrassment, god knows, the way some women were. Her mother's last efforts had been to keep Denise from knowing the diaper needed changing. She called a breast a bosom and a bowel movement "a morning's morning."

Not of humiliation or the loss of prowess, the way so many men were, wanting to die rather than having to be helped to the bathroom. Not recognizing themselves in the mirror, hating the skeletal stranger who'd come out of their Vic Tanny closet.

Denise wasn't afraid of grief, either. She knew what grief felt like, like a knife inside you, a knife that cut you when you moved. But this was ugly and intractable, a monster in her basement, sullen and stupid and deadly.

She dreamed she was dying, and woke to find her pants wet. Richard accused her of "not facing" her incontinence. "It's not incontinence!" she cried out, forgetting she wasn't supposed to excite herself. A wave of pain hit her and she reeled back into the bed.

"No? Well, what is it, then?" He stood over her glowering, throwing down another challenge.

And she was equal to it. She told him the truth. "It's fear," she said. "I'm afraid of dying." She'd been a bed-wetter all through childhood, and even after marriage. Anger was at the bottom of it, they said. Anger was the troll under every bridge. They also said fear and desire were two sides of the same coin. Maybe that was what made this fear different. Maybe this coin had no face, no building. Just an eagle with arrows in both claws.

Richard tried to be kind. He *was* kind. But he didn't understand. She knew what got to him was the thought of all her wasted effort. Richard's parents had drummed the "waste not, want not" business into him in a very big way. "Come on, Richard!" she told him. "That proverb is supposed to apply to food—It's about the Depression and leftovers."

He shook his head. "No," he said. "It's about everything."

Never mind. She more than anyone had benefited from his stubborn, single-focus fidelity. She didn't want to look any gift horse in the mouth.

Her thoughts came back to the package in her lap.

Richard wasn't waiting for her when she got home. No, of course not. That was part of letting her have one last time on her own.

She walked through the front door slowly, her

legs already beginning to betray her. From now on, it would be the walker, if she was lucky. After that, the wheelchair. Then the porta-potty. Then nothing.

She got undressed, looking at every item of clothing, feeling foolish, feeling profound. The dress was difficult to relinquish. She had fished this dress out of the back of her closet—last worn to Leah's kindergarten graduation. What a time that had been! Tiny kids wearing gowns and mortarboards and receiving diplomas—the first of many graduations. Denise had been moved despite herself.

The underpants were the worst. Plain white cotton underpants, size 5/6. She never liked to wear underpants when she was sick. Richard had teased her about that in the old days, the days when they were both young and healthy and intent on the gleams in each other's eyes. What would happen to these pants after she died? Would they go to the Goodwill? Would bag-ladies paw over them? Would they hold them up to their faces and smell the crotch? Would they catch the scent of death and drop the pants like a hot potato, back in the bin? Why did she care?

Distraction—even self-distraction—had its limits in the war she was waging. Denise had gone back to the Catholic Church, the church to which she'd converted in college. She'd fasted and gone to early morning mass and taken communion under both hosts, the wafer and the purple juice. But nothing happened to her fear. Going to mass, Catholicism, was like putting a flower in the dish of a hungry dog.

She was afraid of that dog—afraid of death—not of what it would do, not of what she would or wouldn't feel, or what people would think—she was afraid of *it*.

She tried channeling, rebirthing, regression, mantras and gurus, analysis and encounter groups and desensitization. And there the dog was. And there she was, petrified. Might as well expect granite to dissolve with the application of bathwater.

"Mommy?" Leah said in a soft voice, from outside the room. "I'm glad you told me—about Santa Claus." Or maybe she, Denise, had just imagined it. Maybe truth, like God, could play hide and seek.

Denise took her medicine with the last of the bedside water, then hobbled naked down a corridor that lengthened as she went. She sat on the cold toilet, eked out her usual orange trickle, and remembered to flush. She got half of herself into a robe, then hobbled back to the bedroom and crawled into bed.

She was lying in the snow outside the church. She moved her arms, to make an angel. The priest came and stood over her, the sun was a halo behind his head, and he wasn't mad. "You're a lovely angel," he told her. "A snow angel with red mittens." She didn't want mittens on her hands and began pulling them off with her teeth. She got them off just in time—Richard had come in and was sitting beside her, his white sleeves rolled up in a way that made her resentful and dreamy. She was twelve, on a Long

Island train, alone in the real world for the first time. A businessman sitting one seat up the aisle across from her took his snowy shirt in hand and rolled his cuffs back, exposing a slim but muscular forearm whose thin gold hairs glinted in the sun. Denise the child had fantasies then which Denise the adult could not remember, coded as they were in a language she had forgotten. But they had to do with pirates and Douglas Fairbanks, Jr., who put her over his shoulder and carried her below decks and did wonderful things to her, things she could hardly allow herself the luxury of imagining.

"How was your day?" Richard asked.

"Not that great. Where's Leah?"

"She'll be up in a minute." He had the box in his hand. "What'd you get?" He seemed really interested, so Denise unwrapped the parcel with balky fingers, and showed him the horse. He sat on the edge of the bed, turning the horse around in his large, capable hands. It was the first time in a long time he hadn't asked about pain, or medication.

Richard grinned at her.

"Look inside," Denise said.

Richard held the horse up to the light, looking. There had been eggs like that once, hadn't there? Eggs made of sugar, bigger than baseballs. Eggs you could look in.

"This is amazing," Richard said. "I never saw anything like it before. Leah'll be in seventh heaven for at least five minutes."

Denise struggled upright in the bed. "I want you

to have it, Richard."

"Me? It's not really my—" He stopped and looked at her.

"I know. It's not really your kind of thing. I bought it for Leah." Denise could hear her voice, steeplechasing over the words, trying to get everything said before she ran out of breath. "But Leah's got lots of knick-knacks. And maybe sometimes people should get things that *aren't* them so they... I don't know. It made you grin, anyway. I haven't seen you grin in a long time."

Richard grinned again. "Well," he said, still turning the horse in his hands. "I don't know what to say."

"You love me, don't you?" Denise said, sliding away from him onto a pond. The pond was made of ice so pure you could see your face in it, your face as you wanted to see it, your face as it once had been... She skated back to Richard, who was waiting for her, the gift horse in his hands. "You can always say you love me if it's true."

Richard bent over and kissed her on the forehead. "I love you if it's true, Denise."

She was in the middle of a forest where all the trees were men in black suits, and all the leaves were crows. Suddenly, she found a clearing and in the clearing was a host of wolves and Leah was with her, holding her hand, looking cold and scared. She, Denise, would throw herself down, and the wolves would devour her and she felt their hot breath on her face and she wanted that to be the last but far in the distance she heard a child calling and she knew who it was.

She roused herself again. "Hi there, sweetie. I bought you a horse." Her own voice was a long string disappearing around a corner. She followed it. "I gave it to your dad because it made him grin."

"Mommy?" Leah said. "Do I have to leave you alone now?"

Denise rolled her head side to side to say no. She wanted to tell Leah that "Mommy," was a plate of chocolate chip cookies, warm from the oven, and "alone" was a glass of fresh, cold milk, and nothing could be better than to have them together.

"Are my eyes red?" Leah asked. "Do I look like I've been crying?'

Denise roused Denise, and looked. There sat her beautiful daughter... clear blue eyes... the evidence of tears. Her bangs fell below her brows—she needed a haircut. Spun-gold crescents lay on the barbershop floor. Only there weren't barbershops any more. Just poles spinning red and white, red and white, in the dark December woods where Snow White and Briar Rose went riding, riding, followed by wolves who were whiter than snow.

"Mommy?" Leah said. "I have a confession to make. I said I was glad you told me about Santa Claus, but I wasn't. I wasn't glad at all. Can you forgive me?"

She had fallen off the world and the trees were cold. But Leah was calling and deserved an answer. The darkness halted and the wolves fell back.

Denise opened her eyes. Leah was sitting on the bed, holding her hand and looking worried. "There you are, mommy" she said, with a quivering smile. "Can you forgive me?"

Denise moved a little in the line. The man ahead of her took a gun out of a cigar box. He smiled to her, and bowed, then took the gun, put it to his mouth, and blew the trigger. There was no noise, just a red explosion of silence. It was Denise's turn. She had peed in her pants again. Her mother would be furious. She was cold and wet and something awful was about to happen.

She found Leah's hand, stranded. "There's nothing to forgive."

Leah looked at her, big blue eyes round with fear and fear's attendants. "Are you afraid of dying, mommy?" And it was Leah with the gun in her hand. Denise wanted to tell her the truth. But the truth wouldn't make her free. Only love could do that. And the truth was fear but all her life had been leading to this and love labored and brought forth a beautiful lie and she nurtured the lie and breathed what was left of her life into it because there was no betrayal when it came to Leah, there was only Leah and Leah would believe her and the lie would help her, would light a way for her in darkness where the truth would not. And she, Denise, would give Leah this life, this lie, and under cold evergreen branches, she found a plate of warm cookies meant for reindeer.

"Oh, sweetie," she said. I got to love you... I'm not afraid of anything at all."

A gang of black birds lifted from the forest and flew away, screaming, True! True! True! No one managed to hear them.

RODIN'S GIRLFRIEND

We see her, middle aged, overweight, homely, sitting in a chair

Welcome to Montdevergues, asylum for the cold, the insane, and the inconvenient.

It's November 19, 1917 and 19 was always my unlucky number—I met Rodin, the Prince of Criminals, when I was 19, and the public war to end all public wars began on July 19...

I've had visitors before, but never so many, never so somber. Why, I wonder, have you come exactly now? I had not thought *compassion* moved so many.

Ah, you've been instructed to silence, of course, but anyone who's lived with a Man of Stone knows silence is more eloquent than speech.

It doesn't matter. I'm ready to talk about the *tradable* commodity that used to be my life.

The authorities were of two minds about your coming, you know. They, the authorities, like we crazies, are of two minds about everything. I spoke

24

on your behalf. Let them come, I said. I like crowds as long as they are weaponless. Let them listen. Let them make up their fabulous, collective mind—about me and this barren fireplace, this hollowed out heart at the heart of stone, this locked up universe which some inhabit and some inspect...

You see how it is. I am blessed with the final charities—Confusion and Honesty, two children, hand in hand, before the sister (that's me) went crazy, and the brother (my brother, Paul) turned into a desert son—theological and cruel.

We need a *story* that begins not "Our Father Who"—"Our Father" stretches out a hand to Him, Auguste Rodin,the great destruction of my erstwhile life—but "Once upon a time". *Those* words are soft, white bread crumbs, dotting the tangled grass, luring forth nesting birds from God's stone beard.

So...Once upon a time, I was Camille Claudel, young and beautiful and gifted. I am fifty-three now, and as you see.

I have been *immured* here in Montdevergues for more than four and a half years, since March 10, 1913. They say, because of the outside war, I'm better off with all this stonework to protect me, but no one is offering to trade places.

I did not come here of my own accord.

When I was a student of Rodin's, the *first* thing he made me abandon was my insistence on authorship. He'd have me model legs, draperies, a penis—oh, yes, nothing was sacred—or, rather, it was all sacred, and hence, within our reach. My specialty was hands. Only a fool could compare his work and mine—the work I used to be allowed to do. We both stood by the river, watching an autumn leaf float by: but Auguste tried to capture the leaf, to make it stay, to turn it to a bead of leafness in the mind. The leaf was of no importance to me—except as a way to understand the river. I wanted to work stone in such a way it would exemplify the deepest human dream—the dream of motion, emotion, swelling to release!

The first time I saw Rodin, I was young, and believed in the power of my intelligence to save me. Rodin said he'd devised a "word-test" to see if a young person like myself (he was thirty-nine) had what he called "sculptural promise."

He asked me to say two nouns quickly, without thinking. When I answered, he accepted me as his student on the spot. Much later when we first made love, he told me future sculptors favored an abstract/human conjunction. I had answered "Death" and "maiden."

I tickled his left testicle and asked, "But which of the two is *human*, which *abstract*?"

He didn't have an answer; he never had any answers for me… Ah, but even now, thinking of him, the Prince of Thugs, I've managed to get myself excited.

Perhaps you want me to raise my skirts and explore myself in front of you with two arthritic fingers…

You long for—Exposure—the hemlock of the

sane…No, I'm wrong.

Tonight is dripping with historical significance. You don't want exposure now. You want *reaction*. You came here today to tell me that Rodin is dead.

Rodin… Despite everything he did, I would grieve in front of you if I could, but we dead are notorious for our lack of tears.

You wanted to be the bearers of bad tidings, but rumor cheated you. You wanted to be me, hobbling through Paris, trying to smile, trying not to bleed, arriving at the studio, finding him alone, saying I lost it, I lost the baby—and seeing on his face the scimitar smile of relief—a *warrant* for the *death* of *everything*.

"You don't understand, Auguste," I said, sinking to the only ground from which I knew I could not fall, "I was going to the bathroom and it dropped out, it dropped down into the sewer… I could hear it when it landed in the moving fecal muck."

"You must have taken something," he replied. His voice was careful and it scared me. "It must have been dreadful, poor Camille. You must have thought life as we know it was coming to an end."

But life as we know it is always coming to an end.

Do you understand? *The far-sighted swim in irony-infested water*.

Faced with Rodin, I could never think. His hands would fasten on my breasts like milking spiders. Rodin, you criminal, you used your talent to pawn your soul, but you didn't know when you first lay

27

with me that you were not my first; the thin skein of blood that seemed to give my confirmation to your sheets was testimony to your member's breadth—only that, and nothing more. And when I lied and said the baby that dropped into the Paris sewers had been yours, you smiled. You smiled, and I hated you for being grateful—grateful to me because you thought me guilty of the murder of our child.

"Gross fool, it was the baby of my brother Paul, Paul the scholar, Paul the not-quite priest, so tentative, so narrow and so singular, he hung beyond my reach until my nether opening pulled him in and held us captive in a ring of fire, until he had no choice but to *express himself* in a spasm so involuntary I do not even think he even knew what had happened.

I meant to say much less... Thinking about the two men I learned too late to stop loving has exhausted and betrayed me. I will only commend myself to your good graces and let you go. A little advice, though: eat nothing but unpeeled potatoes, or eggs cooked in their shells. Contamination, like beauty, is so far only skin-deep.

Let me close, then, with a benediction. "Imaginary God, tormenting and tormented in the name of love, have mercy on our souls. So human. So abstract."

Perhaps she kneels at this point. Perhaps not.

FABLE

There was a hare who raced a tortoise and was so much faster than the tortoise that he got bored and fell asleep.

Moral: Ability can inhibit performance.

While the hare slept, he had several nice dreams. He awoke to find that the tortoise had beaten him to the finish line.

Moral: Dreamers have difficulty getting ahead.

The tortoise was happy, not because he had won the race but because he thought his name would go down in history.

Moral: Most animals value achievement as a means to recognition.

The tortoise was wrong: the story of the race survived, but no knowledge of the racers.

Moral: History is more a matter of deeds than doers.

Because the tortoise had been victorious, many other tortoises challenged hares to races: all these tortoises lost.

Moral: One success can inspire many failures.

When the hare's son grew up, his father told and retold him the story of the race, saying, "Where I failed, you must succeed."

Moral: A father who has been a failure is difficult to live with.

When the tortoise's son grew up, his father told and retold him the story of the race, saying, "Where I succeeded, so must you."

Moral: A father who has been a success is difficult to live with.

The old tortoise wanted his son to be rich and famous, so he urged him to stop reading so much and go out for track. Mrs. Tortoise also wanted the youngster to be rich and famous, so she urged the opposite.

Moral: Those with the same goals are often opposed when it comes to the question of means.

The old tortoise threatened to stop supporting his wife if she didn't drop her opposition to the younger's racing, so she dropped it.

Moral: Practical considerations are often of principal importance. Also: female tortoise persons are not liberated.

The old tortoise and the old hare arranged for their sons to race each other—the old tortoise because he wanted the young tortoise to beat the young hare, and the old hare because he wanted the opposite.

Moral: Reverse of #8 above.

The race was set for Sunday afternoon; that morning, almost everyone went to church.

Moral: A lot of animals go to church.

The minister's sermon was entitled, "All Animals Are Equal," but the odds that afternoon were 100 to 1 against the tortoise.

Moral: Odds-makers don't think in religious terms.

Before the race, one of the tortoise's supporters slipped pep pills in the tortoise's water and knock-out drops in the hare's. Seeing this, one of the hare's supporters slipped pep pills in the hare's water and knock-out drops in the tortoise's. As a result, both animals became ill.

Moral: Fighting fire with fire is hard on the forests.

The race was run, nevertheless, and the hare finished first.

Moral: The race is usually to the odds-on favorite.

Immediately after the race, there was a flash flood. One of the hare's friends quickly jumped on his back, hoping to be carried quickly to safety.

Moral: A friend in need is easy to find.

The hare and his friend drowned, but the tortoise floated out the storm unharmed.

Moral: Winning isn't everything.

The End

Moral: Expecting a moral to give meaning to a story is like expecting a post-mortem to revivify the deceased.

by Lyn Coffin
Moral: There is none.
(Fables usually have morals; people usually don't.)

THE FIRST HONEYMOON

For S.J., who asked where ideas came from

We were in the heart of southern France, in the middle of our honeymoon. Despite the warnings of our friends and families (my parents, most specifically), we had not had any fights, and our lovemaking was just fine, thank you. It was better than fine. It was so much better than fine that—well, everything was wonderful. We had time. We had money. We had each other, and long, productive lives ahead of us. Steven was already earning money as an architect, having just started a high-income job with a San Francisco firm. You could see a corner of Fisherman's Wharf out his office window.

I had been accepted to the one graduate school in the country that understood product design. I had already invented my "Nova Lamp," based on one of those little plastic "snake" toys everyone used to have: I had designed a new electrical coupling, and made a lamp of Plexiglas triangles, lit from behind, that could be twisted to form the shape of your dreams. I *knew* that, even as we drove leisurely through the sunny Thursday countryside, on smooth roads we had all to ourselves, someone back at Stamford was getting his black socks knocked off.

The natives along the way were friendly (we seemed to amuse them), and the weather was glorious: high, achingly clear blue skies, across which clouds out of a third-grader's drawing, a little herd of fluffy sheep-clouds, occasionally strayed.

We were hungry, and stopped at a roadside "Bergere" for lunch. The outside of the building was amazing. Even I—who have never known, or cared to know, anything about buildings or architecture—was impressed by the color: the entire building was a lovely faded yellow—the pale, pale gold of an ancient wedding band.

But Steven, of course—Well, Steven always went right for the structure of a thing. He stood there a moment in the sunlight, and I watched him looking at the turrets or towers or whatever they're called, the bay windows with their leaded glass, the archway over the massive front door, and the stairs, curving up it like a pair of stone hands. I watched him as he looked at the place, and I felt a kind of envy, I don't know why. He seemed to take the whole building in with so much more than his eyes. He looked as though he were flooded with beauty.

Then he turned to me, caught up my hand almost guiltily, and started quoting his favorite Victorian poet (whose name I could never remember, even then) about roses blooming unseen in the desert, or something of that sort. I knew what he meant. Steven was probably only the second architect to have seen this beautiful building in its long, uncelebrated life.

We went inside, and were instantly greeted by the maitre d' who, if I remember right, greeted us first in French. Not that I think we fooled him for a moment. Everyone knew we were Americans. I think his "Bon jour. Comment ca va?" was an indication of respect. One spoke French to those one respected. To be greeted in English was an insult, obscure, but practiced.

Smiling and bowing slightly even as he walked backwards, the maitre d' led us to our table. It was in an alcove, by the leaded glass windows, and the leaded glass windows were open. A slight breeze blew in from the garden, laced with the perfume of thriving flowers (roses? lilacs?), and I could hear a bird singing a song like a question. A moment later, as I sat in the seat the maitre d' pulled out for me, I heard an answer.

Over and over during the lunch, I heard a dialogue of song. The first song, the first call, was always the same—the same question, over and over. But the second song, the answer, seemed different every time.

There were other people eating in the room, but the room had many alcoves and was deep and dark, even during the bright outside noon, so the others were more a felt than a perceived presence.

The meal was wonderful, but all the meals I ever

had in France were wonderful, so there was nothing wonderful about the wonderfulness.

Steven and I talked about whatever it was we talked about then—our plan, maybe, the things that made us happy. Maybe we compared our childhoods—the sad vulnerability of his, the small, fierce anger of mine—maybe we decided that he had used his sadness, even then, as a cover for, or a shield against, his rage. Maybe we discovered that my anger had been a desperate attempt to fight against the creeping paralysis of despair. Probably not.

Maybe we skolled each other with mineral water, as we were wont to do. Neither of us drank, in those early days. At each lunch and dinner, we ordered a bottle of mineral water, and asked for it served in a wine cooler. I think this was one of those times when the water appeared in a silver wine bucket, but with no ice. Steven had to explain. We wanted the water cold, yes, but not with ice cubes in our glasses. Ice cubes were made from tap water. Tap water diluted the freshness, the taste, of the mineral water. Even then, he was careful not to say "contaminated."

The maitre d' seemed baffled by all this attention being paid to water, when the wine list had been waved away, but he hurried to do our bidding, to bring us two empty water glasses, and a bottle of mineral water in a bucket of ice. I said something about his being the "classic" French maitre d', and Steven said he didn't think he was a maitre d' at all, but the place's owner, "in disguise." I said I couldn't imagine why someone who owned a place like this would pretend to be his own employee, and Steven smiled—a little unpleasantly, it seemed to me. He said the "masquerade" was "probably occasioned" because a maitre d' was entitled to a tip, and an owner wasn't.

When whoever it was came back, Steven tried to ask his relationship to the establishment, but the poor man only bowed a little harder, a little faster, and said he did not "comprends"; we would please to pardon his "imperfected English." Steven rephrased the question in high school freshman French—"Ce maison, c'est a vous?"—at which the man smiled, shrugged, and walked off.

Steven felt the poor man's reaction proved his theory; I did not attempt to dissuade him, but I was equally sure Steven was wrong. The tone of the poor man's response had been abjectly apologetic. I felt sure an impostering restaurateur would have betrayed at least a little contempt—if not specifically for Steven and his questions, then for naïve and blundering Americans, in general.

Even later, when Steven asked for salted butter, the maitre d' did not hesitate or give us a supercilious sneer as I was sure an owner would. He bowed, snatched the offending butter, in its antique silver bowl, from the table, and reappeared moments later with a plate and a bottle, and inquired of us if "ouile d'olive" would be to our "gratification." It was.

Probably we talked about how great the bread was, even as we ate it. Both of us hated American bread—"Kleenex," we called it. That was part of how we had met, at a New Year's party buffet table, rummaging hopelessly in the bread baskets, in search of something real under the soft, white slices of crustless bread, the pasty, tasteless rolls.

Steven was a little restless during lunch, though he denied it. After three courses—wild mushroom soup, salad with real Roquefort in the dressing, croquet-monsieur—he was more than ready to "give the guy a tip, since it matters so much, and get back on the road." But I was not full. I was not finished. To order a pastry for dessert would have been a flaunting of Steven. He was ahead of the dark, un-nutritious times we were in, and was not averse, even then, to cautioning people like me about dangers involved in, for example, eating maraschino cherries.

I was willing to risk Steven's disapproval, but not a lecture on nutrition, so I ordered an artichoke. The maitre d' and Steven seemed like bookends in their frank surprise and faint disapproval. The maitre d' glanced at Steven—to apologize for what he was about to do?—to get permission?—and Steven nodded. It was an almost imperceptible nod, but it was a nod nonetheless.

It took a while for the artichoke to appear. By the time it came, we were the only diners in the room. Steven mostly stared out of the window or down at the thick, crusty bread he was shredding onto his oil-slick, gold-rimmed plate. I desperately wanted him to look at me, but I did not know what to say to make that happen, so I said nothing.

The artichoke was sweet and tender, and came with a dish of melted butter. Salted butter. Each leaf pulled out easily, and yielded softly to the scrape of my teeth.

I dipped my way down to the choke, and as I did, to amuse myself, or express myself, I placed the stripped leaves around my plate in smaller and smaller concentric circles. At the center of the plate, I placed the fuzzy inedible bristles that guard every artichoke's heart.

The net effect was of a green flower that lay in spiked symmetry on the antique china. The flower lay there on the gold-rimmed plate openly, elegantly, as if blissfully denying it was composed of what had been rejected. It was beautiful, and it was garbage.

When the maitre d' saw what I had done, he immediately stepped back from the table. He had a look on his face that I first interpreted as a kind of small horror. As he backed away, he held up his first finger in the international gesture that means "wait."

Moments later, he returned, and what must have been the entire kitchen staff came with him. There were two men in chef's hats and white aprons, and three in the same aprons, but without the hats. There were two women in plain gray dresses, and a pretty sixteen or seventeen-year-old girl in dark slacks. They all appeared trooping out of what must have been an enormous kitchen, and they came to our table and stood there a moment, staring at my plate, at my artichoke creation.

Then they applauded.

I was embarrassed when they applauded, even more embarrassed when they stopped. I didn't know what to do. I probably said "Merci" more than once. I couldn't look at Steven.

The maitre d' picked up the plate, showed it once more to his admiring crew, and announced, in almost impeccable English, "Your meal—is free. Absolutement." And they all paraded back into the kitchen, all but the angelic-looking teenaged girl, who stood in the shadows a short way off, hovering.

Steven got up. He seemed unsteady on his feet. He pulled his wallet out of his pocket, and took out a ten dollar bill.

"Steven," I said. "It had to have been more than that."

He didn't seem to hear me.

"Steven...? That's not enough."

He looked at me as if I were a stranger asking for a loan. "It's a tip," he said finally, and released the bill, which fluttered down toward a clearing on the linen tablecloth.

Before the bill landed, the girl was there: she picked it up by one corner, and handed it back to Steven. "Oh, no, monsieur," she said, in a soft, lilting voice. "You heard what he said. Your meal must be free."

Fumbling a bit, Steven tried to put the money back in her hand. "You take it then," he said.

"I cannot," came the answer, sweet but firm. "It is free."

Steven looked at the ten dollar bill in his hand and then at the girl. "I don't understand," he said. "Why?"

The girl smiled at Steven as though they were alone. "I don't know," she said. "Perhaps it is because your wife—yes?—is an artist of the moment, and he loves women, and artichokes, and artists."

"But you," Steven said. "You must need the money."

The girl laughed. "No, no," she said. "I don't need anything. He is the owner, you see. And I am his, uh—how do you Americans express it?—Oh, yes. I am his girl friend. That is, you know, the happiness entire."

She was still laughing as she escorted us back out, into the bright silence of the warm, provincial day.

DEAR RON

I hope you don't mind receiving letters from unknown persons. I mean, phone calls are different, right? Phone calls could be aluminum siding sellers. I guess letters could be that, too, though. *Aw nuts*.

Start again. I was over at my good friend Robert's house the other day. Yesterday. I say good friend, though I haven't known him very long because I haven't been here very long. Seattle, I mean. Seattle is *here* now. I think Seattle will be my last here, though my life has been a sequence of them. Do you know what I mean? I think you do. Is it too soon for another *Aw nuts?* Probably. Never mind. It's kind of a hypnotic, hypnagogic little language byte, that *Aw nuts*. Like real nuts. Press onward, Lyn. *Excelsior*.

Robert is a good friend; so is his wife, Meg. Secondarily so, maybe, because he and I were friends first. That makes things a little dicey. The way it can be with a single woman and a dyad.

I had a funny little backache along my left shoulder blade. Kind of where my left wing would attach, if I were an angel. Meg tried spraying my back with some "magic spray." The spritzer felt nice (it was a hot day) but didn't touch my "I'm small but you can't forget me" pain. By then their daughter Sallie had showed up with her adopted son, Bart. You might wonder about where "Bart" came from—knowing you as I absolutely do not, I think you *might*—Sallie was living in San Francisco when she first conceived. And that's all the hint I have time for.

So right there, in Outer Magnolia, right in the middle of Meg's back yard (the back yard, with its rhododendrons and splashy hydrangeas, is clearly *hers*, whereas the studio—he's an ironworker—does fences and statues—is *his*), Robert gave me a massage, while Bart splashed in the kiddie pool with a sucky—what we used to call a pacifier—in his mouth, and Meg did crossword puzzles—*What's a six letter word with lots of vowels for 'Retrograde Angel'*?

I'm not even going to ask if you wonder about the answer. What I think is more interesting is how Meg knew the word had vowels if she didn't know what they were. I wonder if she's one of those people who don't give you all the clues. In this case, for instance, did she already have "e" or "o" or "i" lined up? I don't suspect it of her.

All of this is leading up to how I felt while Robert gave me that massage, partly under the shade of the Japanese-looking umbrella that dwarfs the little round metal table they have out there (The table, you see, is communal), feeling the sun's warm play across my back, hearing Bart pull his sucky out over and over, making this sucky little pop sound I easily identified, though I was sitting several feet away.

Of course, I was sitting with my eyes closed, and they say your hearing is better when you do that. No visual distractions. Sometimes I try to type with my eyes closed, because I like the click of the keys. I love that they're called *keys*, don't you? *Keys of the kingdom* is the phrase that always springs unbidden to my mind. Actually, and this is me getting ahead of myself, which I do more and more these days— **now** when I think of *keys of the kingdom*, I think of your peacocks. The racket of sympathy.

I used to raise peacocks. An hour and a half (to the minute) before I married my third husband, I was crawling under our house, to drag out a dead peacock, because you can't leave dead animals around the living too long, or pretty soon the currently living will be dead, too, especially birds. No, wait. It wasn't a peacock. The peacocks roosted on the roof. Oh, wait. Yes, it was. I remember the feet.

So now when I close my eyes while I type— which, granted, isn't often: I'm not someone who loves to make little mistakes and see where they lead me—but whenever I *do* do that, I think *keys—keys of the kingdom—peacocks—Ronald Sukenick*. Well, not the name, but the *bodiless entity* of you.

But the **massage** is where I was going before I so rudely interrupted myself.

Aw nuts.

I sat in the dappled sunlight, and Robert stood behind me, and after rubbing my back for a while—through my shirt, through my long sleeved and, yes, *flannel* shirt, which I was wearing even though it's summer here because flannel shirts are comfort shirts, and this one wasn't *that* hot, being old and frayed, and my back was hurting, so I wore it.

After massaging me the standard way for a moment, with his amazingly strong yet comforting ironworker hands, Robert turned sideways and slid his right arm across the front of me, at the level of my throat. I felt a moment of panic. Was he going to pull me backward? *"Ironworker strangles woman while family watches horrified"*?

But there was something wonderful about that one arm bracing me, while the other arm—well, *hand*, of course; an arm can't really *probe*—probed the lens-shaped area right behind my left shoulder blade. I found myself relaxing. My chin came down on Robert's forearm. I closed my eyes. I gave in to the warmth-pressure-probing of his left hand pushing in behind my left shoulder blade.

I felt good *(*Okay, finally I've reached the metaphoric *here* toward which I—we?—have been struggling*)*. I felt aware. I felt the moment to be fraught with dangerous and desirable potentialities. And at the very moment (this is where *you* come full-blown into my narrative) when Robert touched me most *successfully*, one of your sentences jumped full-blown into my head: *"It was like the relaxation of a* *muscle with a spurt of warmth."* Then came the thought. No, it's not *like* that. It *is* that.

That's how it is with me and the three stories of yours I've read.

I can be more specific about your work. I don't think there's any limit to how specific I can be. I could say I didn't like the title of *Never*—not in itself, but because you made the title the last word of your story, and that's a fictional technique I became unenamored of and dropped after using it extensively in sixth or seventh grade. And I was offended by the ending of *The Cat*—at first, I really *objected to* your use of *you*. I mean, it's outrageous enough to write a story and use the second person all the way through. But to tack it on, after the fact, like aluminum siding! Sort of like *nuts* without the *Aw,* I thought. (Not really, I'm just trying to be clever.)

The *you* at the end made me read and reread the story, wondering *Where did* **you** *come from? Why would he bring* **you** *in at the end like that? And, of course, then it was slap yourself on the head time, Lyn*—which, okay, did something to justify the ending in my mind, but didn't make me like you (the **you** of the story, or **you**, the author) any better.

And *you* wasn't (by far) the only example of pronoun-messing-with in that story.

I think, you set up your stories sort of like the South American J.B. himself, so a reader can never be *sure*. I think your stories start out in the world beyond intention: they are born in a cosmic swirl of truth, and you slap that down on the page or the screen or whatever. Then you take the raw stuff and mess with it. I think there's a divide in there, somewhere. You, the artist, the cosmic paint-slapper stops. Then you, the craftsman, the messer-of-minds, take over. You make great frames, and make them seem part of the picture, because otherwise the reader would know where s/he is, and you don't want that. I "get," with *The Cat*, the multiple lives, interchangeable, "And not only with one another," thing. (I'm only going to quote you once.) I get that *you*, the craftsman, bring the reader into the cosmic shuffle, with the one word, *you*, using it twice, once to say *you* were dying, once to say he loved (not the cat but) *you*.

Never mind. I didn't want to get into that with *you*. I just wanted to suggest (I first wrote "point out," but it sounded arrogant) that the artist's *The Cat* story ended with "the privacy of their respective books." I believe another story starts with his going to San Jose *after* Denver. (You mess with time and the landscape as well as with people.)

Back to *Never*: I didn't like its "contemporary disguising" at first. I mean, it's a memoir (thanks, Meg) about your parents, but you dress it up in this tricky way. I thought to myself, I could do that. Anyone could do it. Third grade Picasso, etc. Then I thought, It's just no one (so far, that I know of) **has**. Aw nuts. *Slap in the head. The guy is crafty*.

The third story. My favorite. Save the best for last. You ended it with "the end."

47

I know about peacocks, more than most. You really grokked peacocks, with a capital p. Soulful. Demure. Cute. Sad. Keats. It was masterful the way you flicked from here, now, fact, to there, then, future. "The vultures jerking at the longish neck, eyes still blinking."

The dead peacock didn't smell, up close, as bad as I thought it would, but it was a smell that lasted through my wedding. Through my marriage. My divorce. A private smell, rich with decomposition.

There's a Zen koan about two monks doing their laundry by the riverside. And down by the river, in full view, two crows beaking over a frog, still partly alive. The young monk, breaking silence to comment, says, "That's too bad" or something of the sort. (No one reallys listens to what young monks say.) And the old monk says, "It's your fault." I had that as a koan once. Given to me by a Soto Zen priest. A woman. And Sotos don't do koans, that's Rinzai. Made it even better. I got from the young monk's point of view to the old monk's to the crows, separately, to the frog, to the fly in the frog's stomach.

"Something was about to happen that he didn't want to happen." I worked as a hospice social worker for years. Will probably do it again. Maybe. Something volente. "A few lines and voilà, a landscape." That's you, the writer. "A racket in sympathy." Me, the reader. Now. Here, in Seattle.

I really liked/learned from/was jerked around by/wished I'd written/wished you had blotted a thousand words of/ (Shakespeare and Johnson, are you with me?) your loneliness of the long distance lover fiction. Your stories go to calm and squalls and real trouble and calm again. The sacred moment of. Without the quotes. I'm stealing, like the vultures. Like the crows, the monks, the fly, the peacocks. Steal away, steal away.

Reading you, I had the impression of moving many ways at once, as if I were dispersing. It was pleasurable yet terrifying, like a ride on the roller coaster. When I wanted to get out of it, I couldn't. Mostly, I wanted in. Because that was where you were. I think of you as my property now, you know, the beautiful, geometric property I'll never get to see. I am the nonexistent guest your disconsolate waiters with ragged towels are looking for.

If we met, you might not even like me. I would quote you to yourself, and pat myself on the back. And still, it was **Never 77 The Cat**, it was *you* I loved. You wise old man, you.

Yours till Victor Matures,
Lyn

THE PSYCHIATRIST'S SECOND WIFE

Late one evening, the psychiatrist's wife (I am speaking of myself, of course; I have embedded my own character in my own story, though why this should matter to anyone, I cannot possibly fathom) received a phone call from one of her husband's eating addiction patients, offering the wife ownership of a three year old unneutered male Sheltie of championship lines, recently returned to the kennel of the patient's good friend after misplacement in an unhealthy environment.

The psychiatrist's wife's friend Aaron was over for dinner that evening. Aaron was twenty-five, ten years younger than she, and good-looking in a rabbinical way. They had been friends from the moment they met in the Kroger's produce aisle, both reaching for the same purple cabbage. The psychiatrist's wife had brought Aaron home with her from Kroger's, and the psychiatrist had made it clear there was no need for concern on anyone's part, least of all his. The psychiatrist seemed to consider Aaron as yet another one of his second wife's adopted strays.

There had been moments when Aaron and the psychiatrist's second wife could easily have become lovers, but they were agreed on a course of non-action. They knew it was their moment and they made it last as long as they could.

The psychiatrist's wife tried to get Aaron to take the Sheltie, but he pleaded the usual excuses, and confessed he didn't have her way with animals. She openly doubted that, citing his stellar relations with her two dogs and the psychiatrist's daughter. Aaron acknowledged the truth of this but added ruefully, "Yes, but that's only because they don't belong to me."

On a Saturday late in March, two weeks before Easter, the dog they named Shelley arrived. The psychiatrist, his second wife, the overweight patient, the kennel owner and the psychiatrist's adopted daughter, stood and watched as Shelley ran to and fro outside with his neck chain dangling, doing his haphazardly intent business, marking his territory with a vengeance, as the psychiatrist said, to the general boredom of the two female dogs already in residence. It was agreed there was to be a trial period of a week, after which a decision would be made and Shelley returned to the kennel or papers forwarded from there. This much was hammered out in intense negotiations since, as the kennel owner put it, she didn't usually provide papers with freebies. The contractual arrangements being concluded, the patient and the kennel owner took off in the kennel owner's van, leaving Shelley behind.

Almost a week went by without any relevant problems. The dog ran away once, but he was picked up by the Humane Society a day later, or at least a dog answering his description was. The psychiatrist's wife went to get the dog and pay the fifty dollar ticket, the fifty dollar impound charge, the ten dollar boarding fee. But when the psychiatrist's wife saw the dog in the cage, he looked both so beautiful and so frightened, she was not entirely sure it was the same dog. He was not wearing the collar he had come with.

This put her in an ethical dilemma—small, but with manifold implications. Should she confidently claim the dog anyway? Or should she admit her uncertainty to the personnel? She chose the latter course, and explained. The result was half an hour of bureaucratic interrogation, at the end of which she claimed to have recognized the dog after all. The staff people must have known she was lying, but they let her take the animal home without further protest or remark.

The confusion at the Shelter had made the psychiatrist's wife even less sure of the dog's being the right one, and it came as a reassurance to her to see that when they reached home, the other dogs appeared to recognize Shelly immediately, especially the wife's collie-retriever, named Fa by her ex-husband for "fait accompli." As a matter of fact, Shelley's return from the Humane Society initiated a new phase of canine relations. Although Fa had been fixed years ago, prior to any litter of puppies, in a successful attempt to help her maintain her equable good nature, both Shelley and Fa appeared to be blissfully unaware of the scientific state of things. Shelley constantly had his nose under Fa's tail, and there was much licking, on his part, of both ends of Fa. The expression on Fa's face as Shelley licked was a mixture of boredom and satisfaction. Annie, the poodle-mix, moved to the other end of the porch while this was going on. She lay down, closed her eyes, and wagged her stumpy tail fitfully, as if to say anything was okay with her as long as she wasn't required to play a part.

The psychiatrist and his wife decided to adopt Shelley. To mark the decision, the psychiatrist took a Polaroid snapshot of his wife holding the dog in her lap as she sat at the breakfast table and put it up on the refrigerator door under a pineapple magnet that said "Hawaii." The psychiatrist and his wife talked vaguely of breeding Shelley to the overweight patient's collie, Mignon, and of making supplemental income in this way. The psychiatrist was no good at making money or keeping the money he made. The problem had to do with the "sliding scale" he charged, and the IRS. If he made enough money, the psychiatrist told his second wife, he would be willing to think about her wish to start a second family.

The day after next, the dog's papers arrived in the mail. It was Saturday, the day before Easter.

Then came Easter afternoon. Shelley and Fa and Annie had been locked out on the back porch, where

Shelley had been, as far as one could tell from the mixture of barks and growls issuing thence, bothering Fa, and one look out the kitchen door was sufficient to assure the psychiatrist's wife that Fa was requesting to be let in so she might retire to her solitary spot in the corner of the living room, under the psychiatrist's wife's baby grand piano. The psychiatrist's wife therefore opened the kitchen door, and attempted to get Fa inside while keeping Shelley out. To that end, she held his new collar with her left hand, while coaxing Fa forward with her right. What this triggered in Shelley's mind was anybody's guess. But the fact of the matter was, without giving any sign of irritation or stress—no ears back, no furrowed upper lip, no growl—Shelley turned his beautiful aquiline head and sank his teeth deep into the psychiatrist's wife's left hand.

Her first reaction was one of anger, an anger built on fear like a skyscraper on sand. She heard herself say "Ouch" and hated the childish cast of her voice. She stood, blood dripping, and said in a more normal, adult tone, "Jesus Christ." With her good hand, she tipped over a lightweight lawn table and kicked it in the dog's direction. The dog stood in a corner of the porch as though nothing at all had happened. He appeared to be attempting eye contact with Fa, who had slipped behind the psychiatrist's wife and was now pressing a wet nose into the crook of her right knee.

The psychiatrist's wife slammed back into the house. Aaron stood by the sink where he had been washing dishes, watching her entrance with what appeared to be a mixture of quizzicality and alarm. The psychiatrist's wife pushed past Aaron, leaned over the stainless steel sink, and began to rinse her hand, first with warm, then with colder and colder water. Aaron put his arm around her. "It'll be all right," he said. "Everything will be all right." He did not ask what had happened. Maybe he had seen it all. It didn't matter. She didn't like getting reassurances from Aaron. She was supposed to reassure *him*.

After a minute, the psychiatrist's wife said softly, but as if in her own defense, "Would you get him, please?"

"Of course," Aaron said, his cheerfulness, as always, masking hurt, in a way calculated to make her feel responsible.

The psychiatrist came in the kitchen a few minutes later, Aaron tagging behind him. The psychiatrist was in the middle of redecorating his office. He was barefoot and shirtless, despite the coldness of the day. There was paint spattered on his work pants, which had lost both their pockets and were torn. There was paint on his wire-rimmed glasses, his fingers, his chin. He did not look the part to take charge of anything, but take charge he did. First, he produced a box of cotton balls from under the sink, and managed to stop the bleeding. Next, he asked Aaron to look after his daughter "for the duration," then he put on sneakers and a shirt, bundled his wife up in her winter coat, and took her to the hospital.

There they waited in line for a nurse to see the psychiatrist's wife and make a determination as to whether she needed urgent or emergent care.

Finally, the psychiatrist's wife was wheeled into an examination room. She lay down on the kind of bed she associated so shamefully with yearly gynecological exams. The psychiatrist retreated to the waiting room, in search of sports magazines.

Finally, the doctor entered. He stood at her side, looking down at her. The room was swimming. He identified himself as Dr. Hertz, and someone laughed. The psychiatrist's wife was confused. Everything was happening somewhere else. Pain had turned her into a skipping stone.

Dr. Hertz said the hand was especially susceptible to infection because of its compartmental nature. He said therefore he would like to be aggressive in his approach. He produced a needle. But before he could "poke around" in the large, tri-cornered tear at the base of her thumb, he had to pull off the blood-soaked cotton balls. Dr. Hertz muttered something, then shook his head. "Who's responsible for this?" he asked, almost as if he expected an answer.

After Dr. Hertz had cleaned and disinfected "the problem area," he injected a local anesthetic. Dr. Hertz held her hand for a moment while the anesthetic took effect, then began to baste her hand with water.

Dr. Hertz explained that this would be the most

beneficial and most painful part of the treatment, since anesthetics only numbed sharp sensations and would do nothing to block or counteract any painful internal pressure put on tissue by the irrigation water.

All came to pass as he had suggested. The pain was terrific. Finally, Dr. Hertz announced himself satisfied.

Should she wish to, Dr. Hertz said, the psychiatrist's wife could come back to him in two days, when a doctor would need to look at her wound and verify the absence of any infection. She wanted to ask him how one verified an absence. She felt this was an important point. She wanted to ask the doctor—a medical doctor, a hospital doctor, a *real* doctor—if she could stay there, flat on her back, having her hand held, on a bed in the middle of the urgent care unit on the ground floor of the state's largest hospital. But of course she did nothing of the kind.

She wanted to walk but the psychiatrist insisted she get in a wheelchair so she could get the free ride he was paying an arm and a leg for. He wheeled her out to the car and they drove home.

When they got home, Aaron had raked a large pile of leaves, left over from the previous fall, exposed when the last snow had finally melted. He did not look at her particularly, nor make any of his usual excuses to touch her. But he took the three of them out to dinner, paying the check with a wad of small bills, and she knew what that meant on many levels.

The psychiatrist and the psychiatrist's wife smoked some marijuana that evening. Aaron drank a glass of the Chablis the psychiatrist's wife kept for him at the back of her refrigerator. Aaron and the psychiatrist's wife played three-handed piano and sang arias from *Tosca*. Then the four of them sat on the couch and watched the end of Disney's *Alice in Wonderland*, beginning with the croquet game. They sat like this on the long couch: Aaron, the psychiatrist's wife, the psychiatrist's adopted daughter, the psychiatrist.

Aaron left early, kissing the psychiatrist's wife on the cheek and shaking hands with the psychiatrist. The psychiatrist's adopted daughter went to bed right after that, kissing her father on the cheek and shaking hands with the psychiatrist's second wife.

The psychiatrist was, as they'd both expected, too tired to make love. He had to get up early the next morning to take the dog and the dog's papers back to the kennel.

The psychiatrist's wife's dreams that night were full of Aaron. He was dressed in white and wore a stethoscope, but looked like a small boy. The two of them got down on all fours and made love in the wet leaves and Aaron said, "This is a dream of doggy do," which made the psychiatrist's wife laugh.

The next morning at breakfast the psychiatrist suggested to his wife that they might better inhabit separate bedrooms for the duration. He said he needed all the rest he could get and she was making disturbing noises in her sleep.

"Was I laughing?" asked the psychiatrist's wife.

"Possibly," he said. "It sounded more like growling."

The psychiatrist's second wife sat across from her husband and watched him butter and eat his cold toast. Then she told him there were times she felt like having an affair with Aaron. The psychiatrist stared at his second wife with something like interest for a moment, then he shrugged and began taking the top off his soft-boiled egg.

The psychiatrist's wife was finally angry. "Don't you have any feelings?" she asked.

The psychiatrist looked at her over his half-empty glass of orange juice. "Of course I have feelings," he said. "They just haven't been called into play yet."

"I understand you less and less," the psychiatrist's wife told him. "What do you mean, 'they haven't been called into play yet'?"

"Don't quote me to myself," the psychiatrist responded. "I know what I said. If I don't make sense to you, I apologize. But I'm not sloppy with my feelings the way you are. You said you sometimes feel like having an affair with Aaron. I'd have to know what that meant before I felt something about it."

"That's not the way it works," the psychiatrist's wife said. "Feelings come first, *before* you know what anything means."

"Maybe *your* feelings come first, but some of us—I, for example—happen to belong to the cognitive school of thought. I can give you an article to read, if you'd like."

"Thanks but no thanks," said the psychiatrist's wife, feeling idiotic, and betrayed. "I'll be too busy having an affair."

Early that evening, she announced to the psychiatrist that she and Aaron were going out for a late supper, and said not to wait up for her.

The psychiatrist looked at her with unfathomable eyes. "What romance did that come from?" he asked. "Have I ever waited up for you?"

The psychiatrist's second wife took special care with her appearance that night. She and Aaron went to Gratzi's for a splurge. After the main course, she held Aaron's hand under the table. "I want you to make love to me," she said.

Aaron gripped her hand more tightly. "Oh, god," he said. "If only that were possible."

"But it *is* possible. That's what I'm trying to tell you."

Aaron turned pale. "You don't know what you're saying... You're married. You have a daughter."

"*I* don't have a daughter, **he** does." The psychiatrist's wife could tell from Aaron's face that her voice was too loud, but she didn't care. "She's *his* daughter, not mine."

Aaron's look went moist and blurry at the edges. The psychiatrist's wife felt sick. "That's what this is about, isn't it?" he said, trying unsuccessfully to keep her from withdrawing her hand. "You want to have children."

"I don't think so," she said.mThen, "Maybe it is. How do I know?"

Aaron smiled. "I'll never forget tonight," he said softly.

"What do you mean?" asked the psychiatrist's wife. She wanted to scream. She wanted to slap him. She was a bottle adrift on wave after wave of exhaustion, disgust, panic, confusion. An empty bottle with no shore in sight. "I don't know what's happening. What is there not to forget?"

Aaron's smile never faltered. "I finally realize what I need to do," he said. "You wouldn't be the woman I love if you didn't want children, a family. But I stand in the way of all that. I'm an obstacle between you and the future you deserve." She wanted to strangle him. "You've seen this coming all along, haven't you?" he asked.

"Possibly," the psychiatrist's wife said. She shrugged, and pulled out the psychiatrist's American Express card.

Fifteen months later, she saw Aaron at a party. He was married and she was divorced. His wife was at home and pregnant, Aaron said. They had a house and a dog named Max.

He didn't say what kind of dog it was. She didn't ask.

Aaron didn't look intense any more. He looked, instead, devoted, dedicated, devout. He asked how she felt about being divorced. "I don't know yet," she told him. "I haven't figured out what it means."

"Did you get to keep the house?" he asked. To someone else it would have sounded like an afterthought, but she knew better.

"No," she said.

"That's a shame," he told her.

"Maybe not," she said. "He and his third wife probably like it just fine—especially now, with all the tulips coming up." She gave him the smile of the bright and beleaguered. Aaron was clearly baffled. He made some excuse and went to talk to someone else. She left the party right after that.

She had no husband, no child, no lover. She didn't know what anything meant. But Fa and Annie would be there when she opened the apartment door. They would crowd around her expectantly, tails wagging, needing to be walked and fed.

The psychiatrist's ex-wife drove home humming "Yes, we have no bananas," and beating time with her good hand on the steering wheel whenever she had to stop for a light.

THE BUTTERFLY

A woman sat in a clearing on a bright spring day. She was in the woods, in a clearing, in nature, in the freedom halfway between presence and absence.

She sat not far from a stream, amid swaying grasses, feeling the breezes, listening to the birds around her sing the incidental music at the heart of silent happenings.

This was a sacred space, and she was free to come and go. It was a place she knew, a place that knew her, a place that was always different, and the same.

He had asked her what she wanted, and she said, Intimacy. She meant free being together in the openness of a world that began as an expression of love and freedom.

But speech was treacherous, and meaning was the narrowest part of significance.

When she said Intimacy, he had seen greenhouses: plants being tricked and trained into loveliness. He had seen glass walls and hot, wet air, focused lights, and soil in plastic bags. He had seen schedules and expenses and all the mechanisms of managed growth.

She sat in the woods letting the sun tell time, open to the light, to the shade, to the stream that wandered past her and the west wind that played with her hair, and the woods and meadows that stood their ground. She was a creature among other creatures, single but not alone, strong and delicate, free in the wideness and the wildness of God's mercy. And as she was sitting there quietly, a white butterfly came and flickered in the air around her.

Slowly, she extended her hand, palm up, in invitation. And after a moment, the butterfly fluttered down, to the heart of her open hand, and rested there. For a moment, lighter and briefer and clearer than words, there was touch. There was connection.

Then he flew away, as butterflies do, to resume his beautiful, tremulous journey.

She knew better than to chase a creature with wings, and let him go.

She got up and walked leisurely home.

She felt happy. She felt loving. She felt hopeful.

The world was full of gifts, and possibilities.

Even now, he might be calling, the one she felt drawn to in spirit and truth.

Not like a moth is drawn to a flame.

More like a white butterfly, responding to the invitation of a perfectly open hand.

FAILING MAY BROXHOLM

It had been seven months to the day since her husband's death, and she still didn't know what to do with the mornings. The house was clean, the laundry was done. All her accomplishable lists had already been accomplished. She had ginger ale bottles to return, but the gilt-edged clock—their first wedding present—insisted it was only just past nine. The market she liked wouldn't be open for half an hour.

Through the dining room window, she saw her neighbor's front door open. Their seven year old daughter (was she eight now? nine?) came out as if pushed from behind. She was heavily bundled in red—red hat, red boots, red mittens. She stood on the stoop, a red wool statue.

Julie went and got a cup of coffee, then poured it down the sink, then wondered if she were scalding the insides of the disposal. Coffee was bad for you, though, even decaffeinated. Some magazines said decaffeinated was worse. Standing there, gripping Formica and stainless steel, she asked herself the key question, "What would I do if I were normal?" The answer came in a flash. "A normal person would call people—re-establish contacts."

She tried May Broxholm first. They hadn't spoken since the funeral. May would be glad to hear from her. May was always glad to hear from her. May was always glad to hear from anyone.

She was right. May was delighted. "Julie!" she crowed, in that unforgettable way of hers. "I've called you thousands of times!" May had a gift for overstatement, but that was probably good, that was no doubt part of what saved her. People on the phone, people in bus stations, people on reception lines—did they say, "Gee, I haven't seen you for seven months"? Not at all. "Haven't seen you for ages"—"for ages"—that was definitely the proper note to strike. What could be more normal than overstatement?

"I know you're still grieving and all," May said. "But you could answer the phone once in a while."

"I have a machine," Julie said, then kicked herself under the table.

"Julie!" May's crow was the crow of reproach now. "You know how I hate to leave messages!" Yes, Julie knew—she remembered. Not liking answering machines was also normal. Julie herself for the last seven months had been secretly relieved when she reached people's answering machines. She could leave a message, say that she'd called, wipe out months, even decades of reprehensibility. But preferring answering machines to the people who owned them wasn't normal. Maybe she should be taking notes.

"Listen," May said. Ever since she'd started her "late life career" teaching a special ed class at the high school, her speech had become both cheerful and clipped. "Sorry about John"—that was all May had said at the service, though she'd said it more than once, hadn't she? And hadn't the repetitions been part of why she'd seemed sincere? Julie had an image of words scissored out of paper. "WE HAVE YOUR HUSBAND. YOU HAVE SEVEN MONTHS TO RESPOND...BRING A BILLION DOLLARS IN UNMARKED BILLS TO A HIGH BRIDGE OF YOUR CHOOSING."

"Yes, it might be the very thing," May said. The sound of her bright conclusiveness pulled Julie back into the cold stream of the conversation. May apparently still liked to answer her own questions. But what question had she asked and answered?

"I don't know," Julie said. "I don't know" was Old Reliable. You could say "I don't know" to almost anything. John had clung to that right up to the end. Does this hurt? I don't know. How about this? What about here?

Did other people say "I don't know" all the time? Julie didn't know.

May rescued her again in that unfailing, unwitting way she had. "How could you not know about an exercise class, Julie? Exercise is good for you. It's one of the few joys we have left, and you can't be hurting for money."

The last was a loaded die. "You can't be hurting

for money" had in it anger, curiosity, concern—even jealousy (jealousy!) was a possibility.

"No," said Julie. "I mean, you're right. I'm not hurting for money."

"So what's to decide? There are nine of us single gals signed up. We need a tenth or they won't hold the class. You'd be doing everyone a favor, yourself included, really you would."

"I'm just not interested, May," Julie said. "I'll let you know, though."

"If you're not interested, what's there to let me know?" In a matter of minutes, May had soared past irritated, past annoyed, past offended. She was wounded now. A bird flying with one wing. "I don't know," Julie said. "Thanks for calling, though...I mean, thanks for talking with me. Let's do something soon...Together, I mean."

She hung up. Well, that had been a mistake. Best to get back on the riderless horse, though. She called Patricia. Patricia was also delighted to hear from Julie. "How long has it been?" she asked.

"Do you really want to know?"

"Absolutely. I'm not like May." Julie had forgotten how forthright Pat was. It had been one of her most endearing qualities. Probably still was. People didn't get less and less forthright as they aged, did they?

"What made you think of May?" Julie asked.

"It's too soon for Alzheimer's, kiddo. *You* made me think of May."

"Oh," Julie said.

"So, how long has it been?"

"Almost a year," Julie said. She smiled at herself in the gilt-edged mirror over the phone table. She had not said, "Seven months to the day."

There was a pause. "You know what, Julie Adams? You're not normal," Pat said, almost as though she knew that was the answer—the wrong answer—to Julie's unspoken question.

"What do you mean?" Julie asked, trying to keep alarm out of her voice. She was afraid Pat would say, "I don't know."

But Pat laughed one of her easy water off a duck's back laughs. That was another one of her endearing qualities. "I meant how long had it been since we'd talked to each other, nut," she said, and laughed again.

Julie found herself laughing as well. She had thought the answer to both questions was the same. Apparently, she had talked to Pat since the funeral, though. Somewhere in those seven months, she and Pat had spoken on the phone, or maybe even in person. She laughed again, she didn't know why. That was okay, even normal, probably. Probably lots and lots of normal people laughed without knowing why they were laughing.

Julie told Pat about her conversation with May. Pat laughed at that, too. "I know exactly how you feel," she said.

"No, you don't," Julie said, surprising herself.

"Yes, I do," Pat insisted. "You just failed May Broxholm. She's like a class you take and when you fail, you feel bad. You got a D in May Broxholm. That's all there is to it."

"You're right," Julie said. She had reacted exactly that way and Pat had understood. Pat had put it into words better than she ever could have. Pat was normal, so she must be normal, too. Only normal people could be understood by normal people.

"Do you think I'm terrible to want to get married again?" Pat asked suddenly. "I probably am. But every time I see a nice looking man on the street, I start thinking about pension plans. Marriage is a great institution, don't you think? You must. You and John were so good together."

Water was running somewhere in the house. There was a roar in the pipes. It was an old house. People had told her to move. Something would overflow. Something would burst and there would be no one to fix it. She wouldn't even know who to call.

"I don't know," Julie said.

"Come on," Pat said, cajoling. Through the dining room window, Julie could see her neighbor's daughter had abandoned the stoop. She was trying to form a snowball in her red-mittened hands but the snow apparently wasn't cooperating. The girl kept looking at the snow, at her mittens, even at Julie's house, the way people looked at their tennis rackets when they served into the net. "You must be thinking the same thing I am," Pat said. "Well, maybe not yet. But give yourself another year and you will be. It's only human."

"No," said Julie. "I mean, I don't think so. Thank you, though." She said she smelled something burning and hung up.

The neighbor's girl had disappeared. Called in, probably. Not kidnapped. Julie looked at the gilt-edged clock which hung next to the gilt-edged mirror. She could take the ginger ale bottles back now, maybe get some herb tea. Raspberry or almond. They all tasted pretty much the same, and they were all supposed to be good for you. If she walked slowly, the market would be open by the time she got there. It would take time to walk there, time to exchange the bottles and buy the tea, time to walk back.

She had plenty of time, and emotions to burn. Normal or not, it was true.

AMONG FRIENDS

She is telling her friends what happened.

They agree it is good for her to do this.

She begins by saying she went on a bike ride while her boyfriend took a nap.

On the last lap of the ride, she saw a female duck, constructing a nest in a railroad track. "Such an obvious symbol," she says. "I should have known then."

When she got home, she woke John and they sat on the porch, watching the sun go down. "Talk about heavy-handed irony," she says.

She asked him was he going to get a tuner. The piano had arrived that afternoon and sounded a little wonky.

His mother had left him the piano instead of money. He didn't exactly play.

When she asked him about the tuner, he turned to her and yelled, "Get out of here."

Then what? Her friends inquire.

"Then I got out," she says. "It was his house, after all." She is proud of herself for having behaved sensibly.

Her friends want to know is she going back.

She says no.

They ask what about her *things*, when is she going to get *them*?

She decides to get new friends.

She stays with one friend overnight. The next day, she collects her things while he's at work.

She is surprised at how little there is to collect.

She leaves the key on the bedside table and a crumpled goodbye note in the kitchen trash.

She stays with another friend overnight. The day after that, she moves.

A few days later, she starts making new friends.

DANTE'S THREE-PART STRUCTURE*
by David Lawes

**Submitted in Partial Fulfillment of Creative
Writing 304*

In the middle of the Bach B Minor Kyrie, your cell phone rings, you think. You think, too, it's Raitlin calling to say he'll be late, in the coy and somehow triumphant tone he's recently adopted, the tone of someone who presents you with beautiful, suspect things—roses from your own garden, for example.

You go to answer the telephone, but it's not your cell phone at all, which is happy as a metal clam to pour the whine of vacancy into your ear. That leaves only one possibility—i.e., the front doorbell, which also produces something that sounds like a chocolate bird sitting on a chocolate egg, creating a network of chocolate cracks.

But when you open the door, nobody is there. You remember seventh grade and Sheila Mellum reciting her poem for the week: "As I was going up the stair, I met a man who wasn't there. I met him there again today. I wish to God he'd go away. " And that makes you think again of your probably ex-student, David Lawes, who disappeared two weeks ago from the one creative writing class they let you teach. He, too, was a man that wasn't really there (an old boy, if you're honest). You realize how much of an absence you still feel—though relief, too, because it's hard to be a teacher in helpful ways when beautiful boys are in the class.

And then there's Raitlin's lascivious voice saying that the way to a girl's heart is through her back door, and at the same time (you learn moments later) putting a finger in the center of your back so for a moment it's as though his words are poking a hole in your spine. And you half-jump and turn and see Raitlin's face (catching the look there, waiting for you, quintessential Raitlin, anxious—he has entered your house unannounced, through the street door, i.e., he has behaved badly—and smug—he has put one over on you). Then both of you turn together to look toward the kitchen and presto change-o it's him, your ex-writing student, David Lawes, standing in the center of your kitchen dressed to the gills in a gray flannel suit with a vest—a vest you somehow know will have a silk piece at the back, silk lining the thick flannel, and the silk will be silver, not gray. And he stands there in the middle of all your clashing oranges and pinks and yellows and avocados, a slim young study in gray and white. The man-child you nicknamed Mr. Invisible has slid in from the back, and planted himself in what you think of as your kitchen.

And David looks at you with those gray-blue, water-off-a-duck's-back eyes and you have this wonderful silent communication and all the while Raitlin is watching the two of you, peering at you like a tailor through the eye of his needle, or a host holding up glasses to check again for spots.

But Raitlin has the handicap of operating on a higher, less meaningful level. He is operating on an above-the-table, world-of-appearances level, and you and your David are the wife and guest whose hands, knees, whatever, meet under the table, however briefly, in one of the trivial, ridiculous ecstasies life produces for those who are willing or humble enough to accept them.

And then that brief (not furtive but not *not* furtive) spark of contact between you immediately expands into something greater—like one of those collapsing pocket-telescopes you loved as a kid— because you could bring the stars closer with something not much bigger than a pen and the idea of a telescope telescoping on itself made going into oneself, yourself, seem a good and even necessary thing to do.

And as the moment grows, it changes, nurturing itself until it expands into a shared understanding— an understanding that seems at first composed of several small, delicately-adjusted parts, the first being Raitlin's looking back into the kitchen like a child who, when his quacking duck pull-toy has ceased to make noise, looks behind him to see if the duck is following, even though he still holds the string. But by then the moment has become an integral whole—as when your father pulled your ship-in-a-bottle upright and turned it from an abstract arrangement of parts into the single representative thing it was meant to be.

And you and Raitlin continue to look, to peer at the kitchen where David continues to stand. And Raitlin says, "This is my young friend, David. I don't think you've met."

And the recognition you and David share is like a meal with courses. First, you both realize Raitlin's statement is really a pass/fail question which both of you need to answer. You, going further, now deduce what has happened and can construct a model of reality: David dropped your class at the point Raitlin invited him to go along with the two of you to dinner. He knew he could not be your friend if he were also your student—knew, too, that Raitlin would never have invited him to meet you, invited him as a friend, if Raitlin knew he had been taking your class. And as you look at him now, there is a kind of plea to his look, or rather that vulnerable stiffness that a child's face has when he has decided that he is not good and therefore cannot ask something or will not ask something because it is the kind of thing that must be given unasked, or because he wants it too much. And you know that since he has already made the decision to come along on this evening and thereby also made the decision not to tell Raitlin the truth, since he has already committed a kind of proleptic betrayal, not of lies or half-truths, but of silence, you are now forced to choose between betrayals. If you admit having met David, having seen him among your class-ranks until two weeks ago, then David's game is over: you will have betrayed him by betraying his betrayal of Raitlin. But if you say nothing, then you too are betraying Raitlin, allying yourself with David in his silence. You choose to say nothing and this is a shared recognition that David valued you enough to risk losing Raitlin's friendship on the chance of gaining yours—and that he is important enough already to make you willing to match his bid.

And so, you stand—you and David—the two of you bound already in a betrayal of the third, in an outrageously intimate mutuality of feeling. You have put out a bag of unopened chips and the three bottles of beer on the table are still sweating their brown, chill sweat, but you suggest immediate departure and before either of them can respond, there is the sound of a toilet's flushing upstairs and the somewhat alarming whoosh of water in the walls, meaning your husband is at least semi-conscious.

"Après nous, le déluge," Raitlin says, and the three of you leave the kitchen single-file, going out the same way they came in, out to where Raitlin's silver-grey Mercedes waits, engine still running. You gesture toward the engine with one hand, and a shrug indicative of a question you are too polite to voice.

"Well, of course, we should have." (Should have turned it off, he means.) "But I told David that you, unique among women, were famous for quick getaways and one of the several great things about David is, he always believes what his elders tell him.... You and I shall be backseat drivers, my dear, and pretend we have hired this beautiful young man to—" Raitlin pauses for an effect which is none the weaker for being intentionally prurient—"drive us about."

At dinner, David says many pleasing things. He refers, for example, to the wine as "warming the hackles of Raitlin's heart." He makes "litigious" sound sexy. Raitlin looks at you like a birthday party magician looks at the mother of the host when pulling a live white bunny out of his top hat by the ears while all the small assembled hordes squeal with delight.

David asks you and Raitlin what two things you love above all else. You say, not quite laughing, your house and your career. You do not say your friends, you do not say your husband. Raitlin says your house and your career are the two things he loves best as well. David objects.

"Oh, the querulous passions of youth," Raitlin complains with an exaggerated moue. "Can't stand being third runner-up, can you, kid?"

You—knowing you are meant to—ask David what *his* two most loved things are, and he tells you the Sistine ceiling and Bernini's St. Theresa, then adds apologetically, "I meant artistic things." Raitlin reaches across the table and grabs the end of David's silver tie. He mimes pulling David to him, pretends to dunk the end of the tie in your water glass, then releases it, grabs your tiny black silk purse, and dumps its contents—a lipstick, a compact, a twenty dollar bill—on the table. You would be angry if anyone else did this, but Raitlin does it with such deft absent-mindedness, you cannot find it in your heart to be angry. You are struck once again by his physicality—Raitlin is small, with a nothing-special shape, but he reminds you of a concentrated product, packaged with a label which guarantees that in the long run this product will save you money because a little of it goes so far or does so much. You remember a science fiction story you read in seventh grade about a little boy in the future who ate a year's supply of his family's food pills and exploded.

You are fascinated by the way Raitlin and David seem to go together in coloring—David so white and ghostly, Raitlin ruddy. You think of a face or a finger pressed against glass. David is the white dead-center. Raitlin the rusty or rosy periphery, depending on the mood.

You describe an interesting student you have, making it a point to look at David occasionally. This is Lara, the student he used to avoid, her patent and unearned adoration of him presumably having made her an object of distaste. You describe her red hair, her green blue-black Shantung dresses (among all those jeans), slit way above one knee. David looks down at his plate and prongs another shrimp, but

Raitlin wants to know which knee. You describe how Lara always moves from one seat to another and back again, always in the back row—like one of those bobbing ducks at a shooting gallery. This afternoon, you tell them, the six foot four class clown was at the top of his Engineering Student form. He read his latest story aloud to the class, read it against you somehow, and the class heard it with obvious and unattractive relish, as though it were a hot meal from Ethiopia, intended to be eaten with the fingers.

The story was about a man whose wife gave birth to a six foot, four inch baby boy. By the end of the first paragraph, the baby had grown up to be a Swiftian giant named Peter Thunder Buns—bringing home an ox as a gift, wrapped in its own legs, no less, forcing his parents to call him, from the seventh day on, "Mr. Son, Sir," and creating lakes of urine and mountains of excrement everywhere. And such is the magnetic force of Mr. Son, Sir, so devastatingly attractive is Peter Thunder Buns to his gangly, adolescent author that he has to be, like Tolstoy's Anna, summarily destroyed at the end—an Air Force plane crammed with nuclear-warhead missiles obliterates Peter Thunder Buns as he moves toward New York, having mistaken him for an unidentified moving continent.

You try to describe the way Lara looked all the while this story was being read, being acted out. Something like religion had twisted her soft face— she became St. Theresa, repeatedly stabbed. Saying nothing, you tell them, Lara provided our author the greatest tribute, creeping down the side aisle like a guilty thing, moving row by row closer to the front where the rest of the class clustered, a circle of the author's friends and admirers. Down, down, she came and finally settled on the fringe of the group, only three rows from the author himself—an outcast at camp, drawn to the fire by the jabbing of sticks and marshmallows bursting into sticky flame. And, behold, Lara raised her hand, was recognized, and made her first public comment, announcing to the world in a loud whisper that she much admired the author's twisted mind.

You sit back, exhausted, and let Raitlin take over.

You wonder why Raitlin looks at David with glances full of private meaning—the "did you catch that" look you give to someone when a third party is behaving as you predicted they would. What has Raitlin been telling David about you, that you have so obviously confirmed by what you did or didn't say?

How do the two of them entertain themselves when they are alone?

Raitlin talks about famous poets he has known, describes how Frost, leaving on a train for Boston where he was to meet Eliot said, "I have a rendezvous with death," and how, at another occasion, when a younger poet had gone down on one knee in worship of him, Frost said, "Both knees, Thomas. Both knees." Most of these stories seem to be about someone's submission or subjugation, and you think you know why.

You're proud of noticing that David, though

apparently lounging with practiced ease, keeps his right hand under the table for most of the meal. His white linen napkin is draped over his right thigh like a waiter's cloth and he keeps his hand pressed upon and gripping that—knuckles bent, nails digging into the linen. A white cLawes on white sand it looks, except for the few moments when it seems to collapse. When he lets his hand lie, it looks both inert and beautiful—a stranger's dead child.

David goes to get the car and you and Raitlin stand shivering under a gold-fringed canopy. It's raining again—the kind of rain that makes you search for parallels. That's the kind of rain it is, that's the kind of day it was. One of those "reach in the drawer and the whole day's shot" days. Only you still haven't made it as far as the drawer.

While you wait, Raitlin philosophizes about infinite regression. He claims to be talking about the Quaker Oats man but you decide he's chiding you for trying to seem no older than David. "Box" is a square word, you therefore complain, to which Raitlin, in one of his I'm-so-paranoid-I'm-stupid moments, comes back with: "Is there a non-square word for oatmeal containers you two members of the hip-hip-hooray generation have been keeping from me?"

You sidetrack him with the story of the yarn container you made in third grade out of an oatmeal box—putting a paper mache pig's head on one end, complete with a penny in its mouth, and how you filled the box with fat pink yarn, pulling just a little through so it dangled out of a hole in the other end.

That was a case where the tail really did wag the animal, Raitlin says, letting you off the terminology hook.

You sit in back with Raitlin and don't say much on the drive home. Front and back, your two companions remind you of the immovable object-irresistible force conundrum, reversed to an immovable force and an irresistible object. There is something paired about them that makes you jealous. As though Raitlin were Dorian and David his portrait. As though David were Pooh and Raitlin were Robin in pajamas, dragging his bear willy-nilly downstairs.

No, it's more as if the two make up a single character like Peter Pan. And Wendy never really got to kiss him, did she—no doubt because Barrie was gay.

Ahhh—so that's what you're up to. You will be Wendy and David will be Peter. You will rescue him from the heartbreak of homosexuality, seduce him right out from under Raitlin's nose. Raitlin will be banished to the role of a campy Captain Hook and he will hate you. But Raitlin is old, Raitlin is heartsick, Raitlin is yesterday's news. Besides, there is still the possibility of a happy ending. Raitlin may turn out to have a heart of gold and serve as godfather to David's and your children, leading them around on a crocodile as fat and sage as a circus pony—the crocodile, not Raitlin.

After a moment, David turns around to see what you and Raitlin are up to (holding hands loosely, limply, each of you wishing you were touching *him*). Whereupon reality breaks in with its penchant for melodrama, and the accident happens. You are hurt only mildly—a broken nose, a sprained ankle—but Raitlin dies immediately, and David, three days later, when his parents go against medical advice and turn off the machines.

At the end of a long, troubled, and not terribly creative life, you yourself will die—under a white chenille spread in a damp hotel room—still remembering what you have never believed was an accident, still alone, still feeling improbably responsible."

She puts down the story and shakes her head. David's story shows considerable promise—indeed, it's good enough, close enough to what she remembers as having happened between the three of them that x-rated night (except the contrived, break-off ending), to make her feel not only used, but cheated. She admires the youthful brashness of his second person, self-as-a-character point of view, and though the death David has sketched in for her character is bleak, she feels grateful to him for having granted her/"you" long-term survival on any terms. Even the end makes a kind of psychological (not fictional) sense to her: Lana (the original for Lara) told her David had to drop out of school because his Lawesyer father shot himself to death on the steps of a funeral home leaving David's siblings unprovided-for. Still, David's is a classic case of "too little, too late". Plus, he never explained the title.

Plus, there's no such thing as "partial fulfillment" in life or Creative Writing 304. She'll have to flunk him if he doesn't officially withdraw.

Lana also says Raitlin left the college to be with David, but Lana is not an informant to trust, enamored as she is of the muse, and twisted minds....

HER POLITICAL BODY

On Valentine's Day,

a woman is in a bar, coming out of what is still called a ladies' room. She is wearing sneakers, a white blouse, and a tweed skirt. There was a cartoon in the stall. The cartoon showed a pants-suit looking at a closet full of naked women on hangers. The woman finds herself wishing she had been born in Canada. She imagines her mother laboring on a narrow bed. The bed springs creak and the howling outside comes from wind and wolves. The woman sits at the bar. Under the glossy but scarred wooden counter, she parts her knees. She has what men call good legs, meaning when she parts her knees, her upper thighs go with them. The bartender asks what she wants to drink. She doesn't know. The usual? he asks, winking. She nods, though she's certain she's never been here before. She begins to speculate on the bartender's private life. She wonders what falling in love would be like after all this time: she imagines water pouring through a dam. She would like to imagine herself and a group of her friends kidnapping the bartender, just for fun, but first she would have to imagine a group of friends, and this would take more time than she has. The woman wonders what her fingers will be doing in an hour's time. She shifts on her barstool, unsticking her good legs from the red vinyl.

She waits for the future to occur to her.

THE DEXTER MILL

I ran into Elizabeth at the Dexter Mill, of all places. She still had those wide-set blue eyes, and that rich, chestnut hair. She dropped her bag of wild bird seed and threw her arms around me. I put down my bottle of sheep dip and hugged her back—gingerly, I must admit. Hugging her still felt like squeezing a cardboard egg crate, hoping nothing inside would break. All she would say about herself was that she was married and happy, but she caught up on what I'd been doing the last eighteen years in five minutes of talk. I resented the easy way she seemed to soak up my life as though it were unimportant—as though I were a puddle on the counter and she, a big yellow sponge.

We had last made love the day of Kennedy's assassination. I wanted to ask her how long it had taken her to bounce back from that, from the sudden but necessary breakdown of us as a unit. I was in the process of gathering she'd bounced back even faster than I had, when a stalwart-looking young man showed up, and she introduced him as her son, Luke.

He towered over both of us.

Elizabeth picked her bag of birdseed up from the floor and threw it over her shoulder without visible effort. "I'll just go pay for this," she said, and vanished.

My whirring mind was in danger of burning out. If Luke was not-quite eighteen, either Elizabeth had reconnected with lightning speed, or he was...mine. My son.

I made a few inane comments, trying to relate to the kid. It felt for a moment the way it sometimes does in the boat, when I'm not so much trying to land the fish as to find out what I'm up against. Luke made it easy for me, said he'd heard I'd bought one of the new McCormicks, wondered about the gearing. Before I'd even had time to develop any feeling awareness for what had happened, he and Elizabeth were on their way, and I had agreed to break Luke in on my combine the following afternoon.

The intervening hours came and went—plenty of time for me to think up a series of questions for the kid, questions designed to furnish me with proof that he was my son without putting him onto anything. If Elizabeth had canceled the abortion— we're talking about the bad old days, when abortions were dangerous—if she'd seen fit never to let me know where things stood...Well, I wasn't going to try to countermand or second-guess her again. I still regretted the first time.

Luke showed up right on time at my place, and

we got started. He was a quick learner and took direction well, but he was hard on himself and had a habit of dwelling so hard on his mistakes, he sometimes couldn't concentrate on what he was doing.

Afterward, we went inside. Before I could speak, Luke went right for the jugular. "You know you're my biological father, right?" he said.

I stammered something.

"It's okay," he said, staring at his hands. "I was born right after mom and dad—you'll forgive the expression—got married. When I was eight, I figured out there was a missing factor. I went to mom and she told me about you and how she wouldn't get the abortion you wanted. She asked me if I wanted to meet you and I said No, I thought it would hurt dad's feelings. She agreed. She said you didn't live terribly far away, and some day we might run into you. We left it there. Dad's always cared more about that sort of thing than I do."

"What do you mean? What sort of thing?" I asked, bidding for time.

Luke looked me in the eye. "Relationships." He paused. "I guess I take after you in that department," he added.

"Well, what does he feel about your coming over here today?"

Luke flushed. "He doesn't know," he said. We drank our iced but still lukewarm tea in silence a moment, then Luke asked if he could come back for another session on the McCormick. "Sure," I told him. "I could even show you where I hang the key. That way, if I'm not a—"

Luke stopped me with a wave of his hand. "That's okay..." He pushed the ice cube at the top of his tea around with one finger, and shook his head. I thought for a second he'd misunderstood. "I knew you'd say that," he said.

"Why?"

"Because it's exactly what I'd say if I were you." He smiled, pushed back his chair, got up, and started to leave.

I got up too. "So, what do you think?" I asked. But by then it was as if we were reading our lines off cards and the scene was over.

Luke nodded. "I'll probably see you around, one way or the other."

I nodded back. "Sure."

I slumped into my chair and watched as Luke retreated into the bright afternoon through the streaked glass of my kitchen storms, then I got up, extracted the Windex and a rag from underneath the sink, and started cleaning.

POINT OF VIEW PROBLEMS

Jack was fifty-six, Carolyn was fifty-one. Between them, they had six ex-spouses, six grown children, and one hundred and seven years of experience. They both listed themselves as writers. According to the dating service, they were perfect for each other.

He gave her one of his stories to read at the conclusion of their first date. It was entitled "Arts and Crafts". He had written this minor opus, he said, long before the dating service gave him her name. The story was about a pretty young man named Jackson and a worldly-wise but unbalanced older woman named Marian who "wanted to screw Jackson right then and there on the hot, sandy beach, but strangled the impulse." In the story, Jackson managed to maintain a more or less permanent erection by virtue of telling Marian "absolute, straight truths without all his normal ruses." The truths Jackson told Marian mainly had to do with his mother, but for some reason they turned Marian on, and the story ended with the two making "feral love" and reaching orgasm together.

On their second date, Jack asked Carolyn what she thought of the story. She said it had point of view problems. She didn't like the way the story shifted back and forth from the male protagonist's to the female protagonist's point of view, she said. What Carolyn didn't say was a lot.

Carolyn thought that Jack was now fantasizing her "holding his stiff penis in her small hands and using it to trace the outlines of her body," as the presumably not-very fictional Marian had done.

Jack thought by Carolyn's reactions that she was probably somewhat of a prude. He had hoped Carolyn would see beneath the sexual skin of the story the poignancy of Jackson's plight, his struggle to escape his mother.

Then Jack decided he had been unfair to Carolyn. He had more or less been expecting the two of them to fall into mental bed together, but Carolyn was a bright woman, he reminded himself. Bright women, for whom he'd asked the dating service— whom he'd insisted upon, actually—bright women didn't just fall into bed, mental or otherwise, with you. That was part of what made them bright. You had to talk about yourself first, let them get to know you. And not just the pretty stuff, either, or they'd think you were conning them. Jack decided to give Carolyn the benefit of a considerable doubt and, for most of the second date, talked about his not untroubled past. Jack had been through a lot of physical and emotional pain following repeated operations on an inguinal hernia, operations which caused enormous iatrogenic problems.

Jack liked the way Carolyn was able to keep up with him. She skipped right over words like "inguinal" and "iatrogenic" like a flat stone over waves. On the down side of things, there did seem to be large gaps in her knowledge. He saw her as Chaucer's gap-toothed prioress. That led him to an image of his having away at her from behind, which led him to a memory of his last (six years ago!) girl friend who gave him a wrought-iron lawn ornament which he'd first mistaken for a mushroom but which turned out to be a woman bending over. He'd gotten rid of the ornament as soon as the girl friend walked out on him, which had taken just a matter of weeks.

Carolyn thought Jack's pains sounded insignificant compared to what she'd gone through with her recent mastectomy. But Kendall, her third ex, had been virtually monosyllabic for the last six years of their marriage, so she found Jack's torrent of words rather like a waterfall—initially refreshing, if ultimately numbing. She liked the way Jack kept zipping from topic to topic and incident to incident and she got to dart in and out of the weave of his monologue.

Carolyn gave Jack one of *her* stories on their second date. "Tit for tat," she said, straight-faced. The story was called "Facing the Murderers." It was about how the daughter of a woman's neighbor had been stabbed to death by a stalker and the woman was at first unable to make herself look at a lineup of suspects.

Jack found the story more than a little disquieting. One of the suspects—" a real thug with dark, bushy eyebrows and squinty eyes"—looked more than a little like *him*, just for starters. Since *his* story had been about sex and passion, clearly intended to start things off on a positive note, it seemed ominous *Carolyn's* first fictional communiqué was all about death and craziness and a marriage in which the husband, Kenneth, saw his wife as "a boulder he was trying to roll uphill, away from the tomb."

Jack was particularly wary of Carolyn's ending, wherein the woman (disturbingly nameless) "riveted" her husband with a look, and an officious and intrusive authorial narrator explained, "In her consciousness now was the blood that ran between them—a long red river which she, like Topsy, would need chunks of ice to cross."

Jack was not reassured when, during their third date, Carolyn gave him a run-down of what she called her past lives, and made an offhand reference to a number of suicide attempts, at one point waving her wrists in front of his nose so he could see the scars.

Carolyn was disappointed in Jack's reaction to her stories, fictional and otherwise. He did not seem to realize how important a work "Facing the Murderers" was. He seemed all too willing to equate her legitimate fiction with his own "Arts and Crafts," a trivial sex farce wherein unbalanced older women waved young men's penises around. He seemed, furthermore, not to realize that "Facing the Murderers," though disturbing as only an ambitious story can be, was actually optimistic in outlook, testimony to what could be achieved when a woman came to terms with the murder of her inner child. Carolyn had hoped Jack would feel reassured that she was different from the unbalanced, sex-starved women in his past. She had converted late to sanity and, like most converts, was especially secure in her faith.

Speaking between mouthfuls of damp chips, Jack tried to banter with Carolyn. He teasingly accused her of being overly influenced by Lawrence, to which Carolyn responded, "Lawrence who?" Seeing Jack's aghast expression, she then snorted dismissively and claimed to have known he meant "D.H." all along. He thought she was lying. He asked her seriously about the Lawrentian juxtaposition of "consciousness" and "blood" in the concluding sentence and when she waved the question away, several of his darker suspicions were confirmed.

On their next date, he brought her a copy of an article he'd written for the American Psychodynamic Quarterly, on "The Blood-Dimmed Tide: Lawrence and the Mind/Body Consciousness Duality."

"It was Yeats who wrote about blood-dimmed tides," Carolyn said.

"I know that very well," Jack told her.

"I like the way you say very," she said, stirring the coke she had told him made it impossible for her to sleep at night. "You make it rhyme with 'furry'."

"One has to be intellectually honest if he or she writes," he told her, trying not to sound pompous. "You shouldn't go around being so willfully glib all the time."

"Better glib than unwitting," she told him.

"Pot and the kettle..."

"Glass houses and stones..."

They glared at each other and stirred their drinks; waiters slipped in and out of the edges of their regard. She spoke finally—slowly, definitely. Jack found himself wondering if Carolyn had studied elocution in school. That would explain a lot of things.

"Your problem," Carolyn said, making the phrase include a lot more than literature, "is excessive use of the passive voice. I think that comes from your being a scholar." She spat the last word out as though it were a term of abuse, but her correct use of the possessive case pleased Jack.

"Well," he said, "I hardly think a few scholarly articles, no matter how well-received, entitle me to designation as a scholar. I think of myself as more of a teacher. Or should I say, 'I think more of myself as a teacher'?"

She looked at him askance. He rummaged in his briefcase and produced a pack of Marlboros. "Sorry, Jack," Carolyn said, sounding not sorry at all. "I'm going to have to ask you not to smoke."

"I thought you told the agency smoking was okay."

"I told them *considerate smoking* was okay."

Jack sighed and put his cigarettes in his breast pocket, where they would be more accessible. "What does *considerate smoking* mean, anyway?" He asked.

She smiled at him as though he were stealing an undeserved curtain call in a school play. To his Hansel, she played Gretel, in league with the witch.

"Considerate smoking means you do it privately," Carolyn said. A pause. "So, you teach English?" she asked.

That was women in a nutshell, Jack decided. They had no use for segues except in business meetings, otherwise, their trains of thought kept jumping the tracks. "Actually," he told her, "I teach history of art."

"At the University?"

"The prison."

"Milan?" Respect flared in Carolyn's eyes.

"No," Jack said, trying to keep his voice afloat. "Tecumseh."

The image of Jack facing mortal danger, a man among men, faded in front of Carolyn's eyes. "Tecumseh doesn't have a prison," she said.

Jack shook his head. The less women knew, the more definite they were, even the bright ones. "There'd better be a prison in Tecumseh," he said. "Otherwise I'm wasting my time there three nights a week."

"Oh, *night* school," Carolyn said, as if that explained everything.

"It's a woman's prison," Jack told her.

Carolyn saw a picture of Jack in a turban surrounded by large black women in leg shackles singing and carrying plates of food. "No racial stereotyping," she admonished herself, "they're probably all anorexic lesbian accountants from Bloomfield Hills." She was getting restless. Time for some bottom-lining. "So that's how scholars make a living," she said.

"I've showed you my bank book, but you haven't shown me yours," Jack said, managing to sound coy and lascivious in the same breath. If she ducked the issue, he would think she didn't understand and chalk it up to her ignorance, like he had with her Lawrence quip. "I'm a technical consultant for a group of geological engineers," she said.

Jack saw himself sleeping in an underground cave. Carolyn came into the cave carrying a candle. She bent over him. A drop of hot wax fell on the tip of his penis and he sprang out of bed. Beast to beast, he met her, knocking the candle galley-west. They fell to it, panting and growling…"What do you do at night?" he asked, trying to make it an erotic question.

"Nothing that makes me *money*, I can assure you," Carolyn said. She was tired from a long day of pouring over schematics for nuclear turbines. She summoned the waiter and asked for another round of drinks and chips.

Jack felt first apologetic, then resentful—he hadn't done anything to feel apologetic about. "You told DateLiners you were a writer," he said. It came out more as an accusation than a question.

Carolyn blushed—at least that's what it looked like in the bar's watery half-light. Still, you could never tell. Marion had been able to blush, cry, sweat and reach orgasm pretty much at will, in that order, that fast. "Most men want my measurements," Carolyn said. "You want my vita. Is that it?"

Jack patted himself on his breast pocket, just to make sure his cigarettes were still there. They were.

"What's that all about?" Carolyn wanted to know. She fought the impulse to fold her arms across her chest.

"What's *what* all about?"

"You expect me to believe you're genuinely bewildered?" Carolyn looked positively enraged now. She reminded Jack of his mother.

"I *am* genuinely bewildered," Jack said, white-water rafting the gauntlet between capitulation and confrontation. "My bewilderment's the most genuine thing about me." Carolyn's palpable dislike of him slid off her face like snow off a roof. She started to laugh. Jack started to laugh too.

"I'm sorry," Carolyn said. "When I mentioned my measurements, you started patting your chest. I thought you were making fun of me."

"I'm just an addict in need of reassurance," Jack explained, not catching her drift. He raised the cigarette pack so she could see it, then let it drop back.

They exchanged a smile.

She imagined rubbing his shoulders.

He saw himself parting her dark hair and kissing the nape of her neck.

She saw the two of them lying down in a room with scented candles.

They were off and running.

A FABLE FOR JOHN

This story takes place many years ago in the mountainous region of a foreign country.

A man had heard wonderful things about a certain woman, and wrote her a letter.

The man said in his letter he would like to come and visit the woman.

The woman wrote back and suggested they get to know each other in letters first.

Letters flew back and forth between the man and the woman.

The woman wrote and told the man she hoped he would come to visit her.

The man wrote back and said he would come to visit her soon.

He asked the woman to come part of the way to meet him.

The woman said she would.

Letters flew back and forth between the man and the woman.

The day came when they were to meet.

The woman went to the meeting place but the

man wasn't there. She went home upset.

The next letter from the man spoke about his difficulties on the road.

The postmark on the letter was that of his home town.

Letters flew back and forth between the man and the woman.

In his letters, the man said he loved the woman, and would come to visit her soon.

The letters were always postmarked from his home town.

The woman wrote a complaining letter.

She told the man she loved him but was angry he had never really left home.

The man said he was sorry. He quoted travel authorities about how difficult the road was.

He asked in his letter if the woman still trusted him.

The woman wrote and said no.

The man wrote and said her distrust was the reason he had never started out.

The woman wrote and said his not starting out was the reason she distrusted him.

Letters flew back and forth between the man and the woman.

The time between letters grew.

Both of them stopped writing.

The two never met.

A LESSON IN BLACK AND WHITE

Even though I missed her terribly, on the whole I was happier with mother gone. When mother— sweet, cloying, undependably and unalterably mad— was with the rest of us (my brother Nick and I learned, early on, to exchange with our father the furtive looks that bespoke our shame and survival), there was no chance of a private life. Of course, there was no private life worth having then, either, so things in their mills-of-the-gods fashion did manage to balance out, despite mother.

Still, it was maddening, and at a time when father had forbidden us the word, to have her, in his phrase, "palely loitering" about the house.

She invaded our rooms, what there was left of them, like the two-layered fragrance of a sickroom. The aroma that clung everywhere—to the walls, even, like smoke—suggested verbena. Not the flower so much as the name itself.

I have never since encountered that enervating scent, which I think of as the perfumed essence of mother's farouche indolence, her powdery transformation, but I had encountered it once before mother began, as father with another of his failed attempts at masculine jocularity put it, to go haywire.

At father's insistence, I had gone to the town's new dentist. "He's the closest one," father had said, "and he seems to be a man of science and sanity, unlike—" I was terrified he would plug mother in here as an example of all that science and sanity were not "—unlike that strange little girl of his. She must be about your age, incidentally."

Father made an appointment and, as the saying goes, the day which always arrives arrived. I walked slowly down the block toward Dr. Ravensback's, reflecting—in my childish way—that both my parents inspired in me a strangely volatile emotional mix, an amalgam of fear and affection, in mother's case, and of resentment and gratitude in father's.

I was right in the middle of wondering whether other girls my age had such complicated feelings about their parents and, if they did, whether such feelings could be considered to fall under that widest of all emotional rubrics, love, when Samantha appeared. I say "appeared," but really she more or less sprang at me from a large clump of rhododendron bushes which surrounded and nearly engulfed the Ravensback mailbox.

"Hello," she said, standing up much too close and furtively touching my arm in such a way that I at first thought she was carrying out a cruel mockery of my mother.

But, "You're new here, aren't you?" she said.

"You don't know me yet, but you will. I belong here because I'm Dr. Ravensback's daughter. My name is Samantha but you can call me Sam. I come out and meet all daddy's patients the first time. I escort them into the *inner sanka.* I'm like those little boats they have in the harbor—what are they called? Well, at least I'm like that when the patient is a grown-up. But you're probably not much older than me, are you? I'm six, but my sister Stella's fourteen and she tells me lots of things so I seem lots older than I am. Everybody says so—"

Samantha's sparrow-like chatter put an end to my doubts about her intentions but there was still the matter of her fragrance.

"I'm eight," I told her. "Almost nine. It's inner sanctum, not sanka. Sanka's a kind of coffee, I think. And you smell funny."

Then, catching the dark flick of alarm in the wide, wild eyes that stared at me from behind black tangles of hair, I added quickly, "Not bad, you know. Just different. Exotic, I suppose." Exotic was my favorite word that week, largely by virtue of the fact I had only just acquired it.

Samantha latched onto it with distressing alacrity. "Oooh, yes. Exotic. It is, isn't it? Exotic. That's just what it is. I believe women should be exotic, don't you? And Stella lets me practice with her things. She has to or I'll tell daddy where she got them, which is out of the suitcase in mother's closet. Daddy put a few of mother's things in there after she left. She ran off with the milkman. It's called Lure

Blue. Stella says that means the blue hour in French. She won't wear it though; she says being old has made it go funny. It's an exotic name though, isn't it? I love it. You'd better go in to daddy now, though, or he'll get mad at me for making you late."

We turned and started up the walk. I was a little confused by the wealth of information Samantha had just provided.

"Your mom ran off with the milkman?"

"Shh," Samantha said, with a warning look at the house. "We haven't got time to talk now," she continued, in a stage whisper which she could only have gotten from old spy movies. "She didn't exactly *run off* with the milkman. He gave her milk with an enchanting drug in it and then he kidnapped her. Stella says he did it because he wanted to stir her jug of cream with his thing."

I stopped short in fascinated horror. "What?"

"Shh! You know, he wanted to put some babies in her oven. Like the Pillsbury dough-boy." Samantha paused on the top step and rubbed her tummy, then she rang the bell and jumped off the stoop, pressing herself back against a lilac bush that adjoined the walk: her white feral teeth gleamed at me from the shadows.

"What's your name?"

"Tammy. Well, it's really Thomas—Thomas Hardy Moresby." I said this as offhandedly as possible, trying to disguise the immense pride I felt at having a man's name. "But most people call me Tammy."

"Oh." Samantha didn't seem the least bit impressed. "Well, after daddy has finished with you, we can go out back and I'll show you my little cream-jug if you show me yours. Stella lets me see hers—Well, she did once anyway, and it was awful. It—"

I could hear steps approaching from inside. "Samantha…What you said about your mother and the mailman. Is that honest to God true? Is it?"

Samantha smiled a smile full of gleaming little teeth. "Well," she said slowly, considering. "No, it's not true, I guess—"

"I didn't th—"

"It's not *exactly* true, but"—this in a fierce, breathy whisper—"but it *happened* anyway. Besides, it was the *milkman.*"

The door opened.

"Hi, Stella, here's the next one. Don't forget, Tammy. I'll be waiting for you out back."

Stella pulled me inside, a tall willowy girl with bright red hair and an ashen face who exuded clinical smells and was surrounded by an aura of frightening, almost funereal calm. She seemed to me to bear no resemblance to her younger sister except for the two neat rows of gleaming teeth that were evident when she smiled. I couldn't imagine her even having a "cream-jug," let alone showing it to anyone, even a younger sister.

As Stella wafted me into Samantha's "inner sanka" and installed me, positioned me as if I were some sort of tricky slipcover on the enormous swivel chair, I found myself wondering if Dr. Ravensback could have sent his daughters to a mad-scientist friend of his and had him pull back their mouths like curtains so that, no matter how tight-lipped their smiles, everybody could see the advertisement of their perfect teeth.

Dr. Ravensback entered, rubbing his hands together. Dressed in white, with steel-rimmed spectacles, his mouth twisted in what could have been a sneer or a smirk, he looked just like the evil Doctor X who had dominated last night's late movie, the same Doctor X who was always defeated but never destroyed.

Dr. Ravensback stopped rubbing his hands together as soon as he saw me looking at him.

He approached the chair—"Well, well," he said—another give-away sign, those double "wells," clear as crystal to any aficionado of cinematic horror and suspense. He glanced at the chart Stella had prepared.

"Oh, yes. Tammy Moresby. Well, Tammy—" I thought for a moment he was going to threaten my family's life. "—I saw you watch me rubbing my hands together just now. I'll bet you're a very observant girl, aren't you, hm? Open your mouth, please, and let's see what we've got here…. Yes, well. Not so bad, really. Not nearly so bad as it might be. Still—"

The "science" part of Dr. Ravensback, object of my father's praise, turned out to be a large cylinder of laughing gas. Dr. Ravensback talked to me, made conversation, while this was taking effect— "Breathe deeper, Tammy. That's it. Deeper—" of the superiority of laughing gas over novocain. "How much better to laugh than to feel numb. Don't you think so, Tammy? That's the girl. Breathe deeper, Tammy. Deeper...."

After an undeterminable while, the "Breathe Deeper's" turned into "Open Wider's." "Open Wider, Tammy. Open Wider."

And after even that was over, and Dr. Ravensback had given my mouth the "Ravensback Seal of Approval," he returned to our original topic of conversation. "I'm a student of human nature, Tammy. I could tell what you were thinking back there when you saw me rub my hands together. I could tell as if you'd told me, Tammy. But that's not right, you see. I am not a man of sinister purposes, Tammy. Believe me, I'm not. What I am is a man of poor circulation. There—" he held up one large (and unlike my father's, nearly hairless) hand for inspection "—you see that? See how white the skin is? That's probably the whitest, palest hand you've ever seen, isn't it, Tammy?"

I thought of my mother, but said nothing.

"It's pale and white, and as for veins or arteries, forget about it. There are no veins or arteries to be seen...."

He was still lecturing me about his poor circulation when he let me out the door, Stella having vanished without a trace.

"So you see, Tammy. It's not what you thought. Poor circulation, that's the answer, that's why I was rubbing my hands together."

I nodded, but I was not convinced. Not by a long shot. If there was nothing suspicious about the gesture, I reasoned, he wouldn't be making such a big thing of it.

I was halfway home before I remembered what Samantha had said about waiting for me out back. I turned around, half-expecting to see her hurtling down the sidewalk after me, gypsy clothes flying. But there was no one. "Oh well," I told myself, "I didn't say I would come. Besides, she's ridiculous, saying something isn't true but it happened."

When I got home, Nick greeted me with the news that mother was visiting her sister and would be gone overnight. I didn't need him to tell me that this was an omen of things to come and when he accused me of smelling funny, that only intensified my growing sense of guilt, of complicity even: for a long time it seemed, it felt to me as if I had brought some terrifyingly feminine sort of contagion home from the dentist.

When father asked me how things had gone, I said fine. He was not a man whom you told about feelings—good feelings were embarrassing and bad feelings meant either your science or your sanity was at fault.

But the next night, as soon as mother had been re-installed, re-closeted in her room, I told her about Dr. Ravensback and how scary he was. Mother nodded. "He's the devil," she explained. "The devil in one of his many human incarnations." Then, looking absent-mindedly into her large hand mirror, she inquired, "Mirror, mirror, on the wall, whose the wickedest of all?" and laughed a very low, throaty laugh, as if she were the finalist in a Miss Wicked competition.

About Samantha, I was less forthcoming. Mother tried to get "something meaningful" out of me for a few moments, then sat back with a shy, sad smile. "Well, of course," she said, smoothing my hair with her small, white hands. "Of course, she must be like me, the devil's daughter, handmaiden of hell."

That was too close to what I had been thinking. Something about my mother and Samantha was disconcertingly similar. Cleverness was my strength as well as my weakness, however, and I was never so clever as when dealing with mother. So I said, "I guess Samantha is a little like you. She looks kind of like you, I mean. But it's the de—" (I almost said "devil's" but mother didn't like anyone else to use her terms of metaphysical abuse, so I changed it at the last instant) "dentist's *other* daughter, Stella, that's odd. She's tall and thin and looks like all the blood's been sucked out of her by a vampire bat." (I was big on vampire bats at the time, having caught the craze from my brother Nick, avid reader of father's old Bomba the Jungle Boy books.)

"That's because she's a spirit in thrall," mother said.

Mother was getting stranger by the minute. I got up to leave, thinking she had enough problems

113

without my bringing contagion into her very room.

But she stopped me with an imperious wave of her hand, got up from the dressing table, and put her blue velvet robe on over the faded gray house-dress she was wearing. "You must get it through your head, Tommy, that there are only two kinds of women—the basically crazy and the basically sane—and only two kinds of men—the basically bad and the basically good."

"What's dad?" I asked her. "Is he good or bad?"

Mother came over and gave me a hug. She shook her head a moment and clucked over me, but I could tell she was pleased by the question. "Oh, Tommy, it's not that simple, you see. Because there can be any of four combinations you see: a woman can be crazy when it comes to evil men and sane when it comes to good men, or vice versa; a man can be evil when it comes to crazy women and good when it comes to sane women, or vice versa; a woman can be crazy with both evil and good men or vice versa; a man can be evil with both crazy and sane women or vice versa."

I thought a minute. "That's eight combinations," I said finally.

Now mother was annoyed—her annoyance was so normal it came as a relief. "All right, so it's eight. Now go to bed."

"But what about when other men or other women are concerned," I persisted.

Mother gave me a sweet, blank stare.

"I mean, a woman who's crazy when it comes to

evil men and sane when it comes to good men—is she crazy or sane when it comes to other women?"

Mother smiled. "But it never does come to other women, Tommy, my dearest. That is to say, other women don't count."

"Well, what about children? Do chil—"

"That's quite enough, Tammy. I really must bid you a good night."

She was taken away and, in father's phrase, "established" in some kind of clinic the next week. I assume she was taken away—I was at school, so I didn't see it. I had been pursuing the subject of honey-pots and sugar-bowls with Samantha at recess, and I felt sure that had something to do with mother's disappearance.

A lot of things changed in the following days, but not too much happened that was unpleasant for quite a while. Nobody, for instance, said anything about Nick's or my visiting her. On the other hand, almost as if to make up for mother's having been taken away, I found myself thinking more like her than before. "Either she was taken away, or she went herself," I would tell myself. "If she went herself, either she was sane or crazy when she decided to go. If she was taken away, either some outside party took her away or father was responsible." I divided things up endlessly in this pointless, pseudo-logical fashion. I went to sleep thinking in this way; I woke up thinking in this way. It was compulsive, of course, and after the pain of thinking in a way one didn't want to think wore off, the boredom set in. "Either there will be a math test today, or there won't be a math test," I'd tell myself, buckling my patent leather shoes. "If there is a math test, either I'll pass it or I won't. If I pass it, either father will be pleased, or—" etc., etc. It was like walking through a maze, a labyrinthine English garden of possibilities. At the worst, extremely boring. At the best, unpleasant. If it was unpleasant, it was either…. Well, you see what I mean.

About a week after mother's disappearance, father took a whole afternoon off from work, which was by far the more alarming of the two events. That evening, he came home broody—and stayed broody all during dinner. Nick and I exchanged conspiratorial glances which said: Father's getting like mother was *before.* Soon there'll be just the two of us left…."

But as we were finishing our canned chocolate puddings, father brightened suddenly and dashed off upstairs. Minutes later, he called us to him, into his bedroom, which was as close as our house got to having one of Samantha's "inner sankas."

Nick and I stepped across the threshold timidly enough. I purposely pushed him ahead of me into the room, so he would get whatever was coming to us first, but father was having none of that. He told Nick to make himself scarce, which Nick more or less accomplished by crouching down on the far side of father's bed, next to the nightstand with the digital clock that threw its letters on the ceiling at night, so father could tell what time it was without, as he said, "moving a muscle."

Then father gathered me in his arms with something that felt like tenderness and positioned me on top of the dresser he'd had someone build especially for him. It was much taller than a normal dresser, just under seven feet, I would imagine. It was narrow—a normal drawer's width wide—and painted yellow, but the special thing about it was this: father had had it built so the first four drawers up from the floor weren't drawers at all, but only fronts for drawers—fronts with nothing, or, rather, nothing but wood, behind them. I asked him once about this and he responded with one of those flashes of literary wit he was apt to use, and which I never understood until years later: "I choose never to stoop."

"But why did you have to have them be *fake* drawers?" I persisted, very much aggrieved. "If they'd been real, I could have—I mean, Nick and I could have— put some of our toys or clothes in them and then we'd have more room in our room. He smiled a funny little smile down at me and said, "Exactly."

He was wearing that same smile now. It was a smile I had come not so much to dislike as to be suspicious of—a smile that seemed almost painted on, a Humpty-Dumpty smile like the kind of crack a hard-boiled eggshell made when you tapped the egg neatly on the kitchen counter.

"Come on, Tommy. What are you waiting for? I promised to catch you."

117

The room stopped spinning for a moment. My father stood straight across from me. His blue eyes—which I connected with marbles, dead fish, and broken toasters—met mine head on for the first and last time. It was a bracing, but not tremendously enjoyable experience.

"Come on, Tommy. Jump. Eric won't let you down."

Even having bologna sandwiches for dinner two nights in a row hadn't bothered me as much as did father's new habit, which had manifested itself at about the same time as the bologna, of referring to himself in the third person. He had decided, he said, not to let either me or Nick call him father any more. Not father. Not dad or daddy. Especially not pop, pops, or poppa. "Those words are out, do you hear me? Out." We heard him.

I had tried all day, but I couldn't bring myself to call him Eric. Nick seemed to like being on a first-name basis with father, though it was always hard to tell about Nick. But in what was to become one of my dominant life patterns, I used my superior intelligence to solve a unique and admittedly peculiar bind and took to calling father "sir." Nick made fun of this practice but only behind my father's back, where it didn't count. The assorted adults that had drifted through our house the last two days had been impressed with my daughterly respect, I think, and father had pronounced himself more than satisfied.

I caught sight of Nick out of the corner of my

eye. He had settled down and was now sitting, in father's phrase, "like a mushroom," behind the far bed. There was an eagerly expectant and yet unfocused look on his face: already, at just-eight, Nick had established himself as one of the world's great watchers.

I sighted down the vast yellow front of the dresser. That was when I noticed the big white bearskin rug that we'd always kept in front of the fireplace for mother to sit on, when she could be persuaded to sit with us. It now covered the distance between the dresser and father's bed. Father was standing right in the middle of the bear's back, which appeared from my dizzying height to be frozen in flat-out pursuit of Nick.

But if Nick's talent was already for watching, mine was already for suspicion. I was suspicious of everybody and everything, particularly everybody. One theory I later developed as to the formation of my possibly premature suspiciousness focused on my having seen "The Miracle Worker" over and over again the one time it had come to our town. In this movie, a very young Annie Sullivan tries to dun it into her blind deaf and dumb protégé, the future Helen Keller, that there is a word, a label, for everything. "It has a name. It has a name," she says over and over again—and finally, with water, little Helen manages to see the light. Metaphorically speaking, of course.

Well, that phrase "It has a name, It has a name" haunted me for days the way any verbal formulation is apt to when it's close, but not exactly right. If I'm trying to think of Mandrake, the Magician, for example, and I come up with Marmaduke, Marmaduke will haunt me until I get it right—until one day in the supermarket when I'm handing the checkout boy a jar of marmalade, I'll suddenly look him straight in his blank blue eyes and say, "It's not Marmaduke at all, is it? It's Mandrake—that's what I've been trying all along to think *of—Mandrake..."*

It was just like that, only more so, with Miss Sullivan's "It has a name, It has a name." And, sure enough, the night after mother vanished while I was doing the dishes with Nick—I washed and he dried—I heard a song which repeated this phrase: "To everything—Turn, Turn— there is a season— Turn, Turn...." And suddenly I was struck, as if with a vision: Whenever anybody did something for me or asked me to do anything for them or even, as now, with my father's command to jump, it was as though a little black voice—black because it had lately issued forth from the thirty-seven little black holes of a telephone mouthpiece—a little black voice seemed to whisper to me over and over, exactly in Annie Sullivan's urgent, instructive tones "It has a reason. It has a reason."

So, while my father continued to tell me to jump, and Nick continued to hunker in the corner, and I found myself staring down at the rug, I heard again "It has a reason." The rug's being between the dresser and the bed—"It has a reason." And the reason? It is there to cushion a fall. But my father is a strong man. He will have no trouble catching me. Or *would* have no trouble, if he really means to catch me. But my father is calling me Tommy. This is a term of affection when he uses it. *It has a reason.* After I called him "sir" the first time, he called me Tommy, but after that, ever since the bologna dinners, it's been regular old Tammy. The special name has a special reason: father doesn't intend to catch me.

I am confused. I can't jump now, but I can't not jump either. Suppose I'm wrong? I began to cry— Sometimes, I've noticed, tears have a way of washing out impossible contradictions.

And so it is now. Father stops smiling and lifts me down. "Okay," he says wearily. "Okay. Go to your room."

I do so gratefully, without any backtalk. I am full of a sense of pain or evil, nearly avoided.

I expect Nick to follow me out of the room, but he doesn't. I step around the half-open door into the hall, and squint through the crack. Nick is standing in front of father. "I'll do it, dad," he says.

I expect father to reprimand Nick for not calling him Eric, but he doesn't. "You would," father says after a pause. Then he lifts Nick up. Without a second's hesitation, Nick jumps. Father almost catches him, or seems almost to catch him. When Nick lands spread-eagled on the rug, father makes a funny gargling sound, then bends and scoops Nick up, cradling him to his chest. I creep off to our room, feeling ashamed.

But this is not to be the end of the incident. Sometime later, Nick slinks in. I hate it when he looks like this: all thin and weaselly, gray around the eyes and mad in that creepy crawly way of his. He's not mad at father, I discover—he's mad at me. "If you'd just jumped, everything would have been okay," he keeps saying. Finally I can't take it anymore.

"No, it wouldn't have been okay. Because father wasn't planning to catch me. It just would have been me that landed on the rug instead of you....Are you okay, incidentally?"

"Yeah, I'm okay...." Nick considers, again in that maddeningly slow way of his. "Well, maybe you're right. But then you should have told me—should have warned me—not just gone off like that." He is hitting closer to home now.

"Jesus," I say, "you act like I was the one who let you fall. If I were you, I'd try getting mad at da—at your buddy *Eric.* Or your own dumb self for being so stupid."

"It wasn't his fault," Nick said. His voice was like pumpkin pie-filling before it cools. "Besides, he did it for a good reason. He told me. He wanted to teach us not to trust anybody."

I punched up my pillows and stretched out on the bed. "Well, did you learn your lesson? Did he teach you not to trust anybody?"

"Yes and no," came the slow response. "I learned my lesson okay, but he wasn't exactly the one who taught it to me."

I should have known better than to think that Nick would let a grudge like that rest; I should have, but I didn't...."

Two days later, I discovered the loss: a little white china pitcher mother had given me, the center and most-prized ornament on my knickknack shelf. I went wailing through the house. Nick was reading comic-books in the living room. I was already virtually certain he was the culprit, and the fact he'd taken his precious comics downstairs to read made him even more of a target of suspicion.

But why the living room? I looked wildly around, feeling Nick watching me out of the corner of his eye. *It has a reason. It has a reason.* Then I noticed the bearskin rug. Nick had asked Eric the night before if he could bring it back down to the living-room and Eric had agreed. The pitcher was white. The rug was white. It lay stretched out in front of me like a big white stain on the wine-colored flagstones. And then I knew...

I walked slowly across the room, trembling violently at every step. When I got to the rug, I knelt down. Sure enough, the bear's black mouth was full of jagged white pieces—as though the bear had choked on his own teeth—a secret, double, inner set of teeth. Broken white china hidden in a black mouth hidden in a sea of white fur.

Somehow, it wasn't the hostility of Nick's act that disturbed me, as much as the neatness: to have found the pitcher broken would have been tolerable, though upsetting. But to see the jagged pieces carefully fitted into that velvety ursine cavity was infinitely worse. And something else was adding its weight to the evil, the pain I felt: I didn't know what it was until I dropped the pitcher pieces in the nearest wastebasket.

The green wastebasket that normally stood by the fireplace was nowhere to be seen. In its place stood the one from father's study. And the moment I stood over it and let the white china-fragments go, I knew why the switch had been made: this wastebasket was black. Again, I was staring down into a black hole, seeing jagged white fragments.

Now I was shaking violently. I couldn't keep my voice from rising as I turned to face Nick. He'd abandoned all pretense of reading and was sitting on the sofa, smirking openly.

"Why? Why'd you do it, you little twerp!" I was furious at myself for not being able to come up with a more damning word.

"Why? You know why. When you knew Eric was going t—"

I bit my lip to keep from crying out. "I don't mean *why* why, stupid. I mean why exactly *this?* Why'd you have to break exactly that pitcher?"

Nick smiled. His gestures seemed older to me, his voice deeper. "You gave me the idea, actually. You and your friend Sam, with all that nutsy-cuckoo talk you do at recess about mailmen and jugs of cream."

I was outraged. "You damn sniveling brat. Have you been eavesdropping on us? Have you?"

"So what if I have?"

But he'd given in too easily, hadn't been nearly defensive enough. Besides, at recess his class was kept on the other side of the yard from ours...But then how?

As though he'd read my mind, Nick giggled. "Why don't you wise up, *Tommy?* Your friend Sam told me all about it—in fact, she tells me everything. She invites me over, too. Yesterday she took me into this room they have in her garage and she let me touch her and—"

But I couldn't stand any more. I hurled myself across the room....

The next few moments are a blank in my mind. All I know is, when I snapped back into being me, I was sitting astride Nick's bony chest, both of us were sweaty, and a thin strand of red was coming from the corner of his mouth. I thought at first it was a string or a long piece of hair—red hair, like Stella had.

"Say it isn't true, Nicholas. You say it isn't true or I'm going to beat you black and blue." The rhyme sounded wrong to my ears—odd, and strangely discordant. But it was too late to take back anything.

"Okay. It isn't true."

"No. Say, 'It isn't true that Samantha told me about...about anything, and she didn't let me touch her anywhere.' "

"It isn't true that Samantha told me anything and I didn't touch her anywhere."

Grudgingly, I let him up. "You're a nasty little twit, Nicholas Moresby. And you're going to grow up to be an evil, evil man, just like daddy."

Nicholas stood and brushed himself off. The moisture on his face had formed itself into a moustache and he licked this off with the tip of his tongue. "Well, so what if I am? If da—*Eric*—is bad, I don't see what's so wrong with that. He takes care of us pretty good, doesn't he? And besides, *you're* going to grow up crackers, like you-know-who!"

I thought of attacking him again, but I was too tired. I wanted to ask if mother had told him her theory, but was afraid of the answer. Besides, the mood he was in, Nick would say whatever he thought would annoy me.

Nick stuck out his tongue somewhat inconsequentially, then turned and walked to the doorway. On the threshold, he turned back—already, then, he was practicing the art of theatre, for which he was to become so famous. A pause for effect, and then, "You know how I said it wasn't true? Well, maybe it wasn't true, but it happened *anyway,* so there. All of it."

When I chased him up the stairs in response, he vanished into mother's room and locked the door. I was furious and gleeful both, sure that father would punish him for his trespass. But when father came home minutes later, and I told him about Nick's being in there, father only laughed. "Where were you this morning, Tammy? I *told* Nick to move in there— to sleep there until your mother gets back. If ever."

"But—" I turned and sure enough, there was Nick sidling down the stairs as triumphant and wicked as ever. "Why don't *I* get mother's room? I'm the *girl."*

Father smiled not very pleasantly. "I'm well

aware that you're the girl, Tammy. That's exactly why….Your mother's room was always meant to be a boy's room. You don't think she meant those cowboys and such for herself, do you? This way, you'll both have a little breathing space and, who knows, maybe by the time your mother gets back from the clinic, she'll want to move in with me. Stranger things have happened."

I gave it one last try. "But I'm the oldest. I should get the big room."

"Look, Tammy. Don't blame me for that. I agree with you. I told your mother to wait until you actually put in an appearance. But she was so sure you were going to be a boy—" He shook his head. "You know how your mother is. She was sure about a lot of things then, and when events disproved her, she didn't take it kindly. How do you think you got the name Thomas, after all?

Thomas Hardy Moresby, it's a hell of a cross for any girl to bear. If you want to someday, we can change it officially to Tammy….Now. Would you mind letting me get my coat off so I can rustle us up some dinner? How do the two of you feel about bologna sandwiches for a change?"

That night, Nick and I went up to bed together as usual, but for the first time, he turned off at mother's room and stood in the doorway (posing on the threshold again!) smirking. I could feel him smirking all the way down the hall. Finally, I couldn't stand it any more.

I whirled around. "You're evil, Nicholas. Evil, evil,

evil."

He sniggered. "And you're crackers, Tammy. Crackers. Bonkers. Nuts." He smirked that knowing smirk of his. "You and your little cream-pots. That's all girls ever think about, isn't it, creampots and milkmen....Well, I don't give a—for your cream-pots." He extended his middle finger upward for punctuation.

I was shocked, and therefore more than a little impressed. "The devil's going to get you good, Nicholas Andrew Moresby!"

"And the men in white coats are going to come for you, Thomas Hardy—"

I slammed the door behind me just in time, comforting myself enormously with the thought that Nicholas's dire prediction applied not to me but to a writer who was dead, and a man to boot. Also with the decision that as soon as I was old enough, I'd change my name. Not to Tammy, of course (Tammy was awful, like "contaminated") but to something altogether different—something unassailably pure, unarguably sane, undoubtedly feminine.

"Virginia" sprang unbidden to my mind but I hastily rejected that and settled on Abigail.

Virginia was my mother's name.

FALLING OFF THE SCAFFOLD

Dear Sir:

I am enrolling in your correspondence course. Yours is the only ad that doesn't take a "writer's cheerleader" approach—"You too can write a sentence that sells," etc. I feel that someone who advertises his services in such a curt, laconic, or at least a "no nonsense" way may perhaps have something to offer me. I would appreciate your not sending me the customary 'credentials' sheet, incidentally. I'm sure your credentials are excellent; if not, I have enough for both of us. My check and my first submission (*At the Museum*) are enclosed.

Very truly yours,

e. trace

At the Museum
At the museum, looking at the mummy,
I think about mortality.
I think about
The hieroglyphs
Slow time has inscribed

On my moving face.
How did you feel,
Egyptian man?
You had long fingers,
Did you play the harp,
Cast the sticks, 132
Or were you a card shark?
The bones tell no story.
The linen, dissolving,
Tells no story.
I don't want it this way,
All up to the imagination!
Couldn't you have left a letter,
A suicide note
(All letters, poems, are ultimately suicide notes)
Saying
I was a painter of pyramids.
I got careless.
One day I fell off the scaffold
And got a fungus
And that fungus
Ate me up. I just shriveled away and
Died. But before I died, I picked out my favorite
Pots and knives and beads and here I am.
That's how I died, that's the way you see me.
Well, that would make me feel much better,
I could even get into that painter's trip,
Feel the scaffold slip—
The sudden drop, the scream—
Perhaps I'd die
And wouldn't you wonder

Seeing me curled up next to the mummy
In my turtleneck and bell-bottoms?

Dear Mr. or Ms. Trace:

Welcome to the course! My salutation is not meant to offend you in any way—merely to point out that presently I exist in a state of unawareness as to your gender, if I may put it that way.

Taking your most interesting and intriguing letter point by point (which is something I believe very strongly in doing), I feel that I must in all honesty admit that it was not considerations of verbal economy alone which led me to make my ad short and sweet. I'm sure you know what I mean!

As for the matter of credentials, I believe you spoke of having credentials enough for both of us. Well, all I have to say to that is, you must have quite a few! Seriously, I would like to know something about you—your gender, of course, as I mentioned above—but that's just a beginning. The more I know about you, the more I can help you realize your own individual talent, and that's what we're both concerned with at this point, right?—Naturally, I don't expect you to tell me all the intimate details of your personal life at least not yet!—as interesting as those details may be! But if you could tell me a little bit about the kind of education you've had, the kinds of things you're interested in writing about, etc., etc., I'd be in a much better position to advise you.

I'll bet you're wondering at this point just what I thought of *In the Museum*. Okay. Well, on the whole,

I thought it was excellent. Really excellent. I just have a couple of points I'd like to make. First of all, I think you might be better off, if you're going to write poetry, to work within more or less traditional forms for a while.

The poem as it is is too strung out, so to speak. I'm not sure that you have the poetic control (yet!) which one needs if one is going to write free verse. So that's one suggestion I'd like to make, that you try something in meter. Now, of course, I don't know (hint hint) what you know about matters of prosody. If you're interested, I can recommend several books on the subject, one of which I wrote myself!

Another thing. I think you run into a point-of-view problem at the end of the poem, when you address someone ("And wouldn't you be surprised") and the reader can't tell exactly who that someone is. Up to that point, remember, the poet-you has been speaking directly to the mummy (I think that's one of the best things about the poem, that use of direct address!), so when you (the poet) say, "And wouldn't you be surprised," I don't think you can complete the line as you do, by saying, "Seeing me curled up here next to the mummy."

As for the beginning, my honest feeling is that it should be cut! ("I think about mortality" is particularly bad. In poetry, especially, one has to "show—don't tell."*) I don't think you really hit your stride until the ninth or tenth line.

To sum it all up, I think you ought to try being less casual, less prosaic, as it were—assuming you still want to stick to poetry after all my discouraging comments!

I'm looking forward to your next submission and (one last reminder) to learning more about you.

Happy writing!
K. C. Jedenacht

* Ditto, the line about all poems and letters being suicide notes. You're perfectly right, of course, but being right is not at all the same as being poetic!

K.C.J.

Dear Prof. Jedenacht:

Thank you for your letter. I agree with everything you said about the poem. I disagree with everything else. I am enclosing my poetic response to your poetic suggestions.

Very truly yours,
evelyn trace

The Catch

I swam the long sea
Down, a silver flash in deepest
Leagues of green, lifted by the swell
And surge, the strong, the sure, the slowly-rising
Tide.Exposed to seizures by a sudden ebb, your bare
Hands had me. I was cruelly beached. I dully thudded
Out my life against your bones and body strand-was
Cut, slit open by a most incisive blade. My Death
Was spasmodic-I labored like a girl
In frank breech birth.

133

Dear Ms. Trace:

Well, I must say that your second letter (?) intrigued me even more than the first! (And that's saying a lot!) As you will note by the salutation, I took your advice about trying to learn about you through your poems. Putting together some of the more obvious, shall we say, phrasings of your latest poem ("I was slit, cut open by your most incisive blade" and so on) with the name "Evelyn," I have come to the conclusion that you are a female-type person.

Also, judging from your address, you live in the suburbs. Going on the assumption that most women (your poems and letter are far too mature for a girl to have written them) who live in the suburbs are married and have a husband and children, I have concluded nothing less than that you are a married woman and a suburban mother! (How am I doing so far?)

As for the poem itself, I thought it was excellent, a real step up from the museum piece (if I may so phrase it)! *The Catch* shows a lot of thought and poetic craft. Still, it's not exactly the kind of thing I had in mind for you. The fish-shape, which (stupid me) I didn't see at first, represents an extremely ingenious bit of spatial engineering, of course, but I'm afraid emblem poems went out of style with Geo. Herbert and his bunch (c. the 1590's) and haven't come back in since! Seriously, I'm afraid you suffer, as so many others of us do, from what I call "the curse of cleverness."

And, again, it seems to me, the poem takes too long to get off the ground. (Metaphorically speaking, of course!) One last thing: I seem to remember your using a phrase like "my moving face" in your Museum poem. In *Catch*, you have words like "seizures" and "incisive" and "frank" and phrases like "had me," all of which are, it seems to me, more or less in the nature of puns. Perhaps you pun unconsciously, perhaps not. (My mother was a great one for unconscious puns. I remember she told me once she ironed her underwear because "I want my drawers to look neat.")

Anyway, I think you ought to seriously consider how much, if at all, you want to use puns in a serious piece of writing. To sum it all up, I would suggest your trying to write a more or less regular poem for your next submission, something I'm very much looking forward to reading.

Good luck,
"Sherlock" Jedenacht

Dear Sir:

Just a few items of possible interest: A) I agree with your criticisms of *The Catch*; B) "Evelyn" is a name which most authorities consider proper for either males or females; C) As so many other poets do, I "suffer from" a tendency to use personae in my work, a tendency which I should think you, as a detective if not as a fellow writer, would do well to keep in mind; D) George Herbert (1593-1633).

Enclosed is my latest submission. The puns are quite deliberate.

Very truly (and pseudonymously) yours,
e.d.t.

Presentation

Fluidly, they draw me out; I take it as it goes.
They wrap my genitals with white so nothing manly shows.
And in the padlock of my hands they place a waxy rose.
In covered wagons, peasant-like, they horse me to my room.
They let me down. I come to terms, assume a studied pose.
Like backward dogs, they shower dirt. They fill me in on
   doom.

Dear Evelyn,

Well, as you can see from the salutation, I still haven't given up on the idea that we can be friends (even if you do seem insistent upon regarding me from the "height of an unwritten book"!).

Actually, I never really thought about you as a suburban housewife at all: I just said that as a kind of test. Even if I hadn't been sure before, the phrase "so nothing manly shows" would have clued me in as to the true state of things.

Anyway, about the poem itself. I think it's fairly good. Your rhymes are a trifle sophomoric, but perhaps that is a good thing, given the subject with which the poem attempts to deal. I really object to two things: your use of puns, about which I cautioned you in my last letter, and which I really feel you would do well to avoid; and, second, the nebulous nature of what you like to call the "persona" of your work.

Expressions like "draw me out", "take it as it goes", "let me down", "come to terms"—all of these plays on words seem to me unfortunately chosen. You said in your letter that all your puns were deliberate, however, so this may just be one of those things we're going to have to agree to disagree about!

As for the "persona"—beyond the fact that the speaker of the poem is a dead man, the reader knows nothing about him. Also, with the one possible exception of the phrase "padlock of my hands" (the meaning of which I'm afraid escapes me), I see little or no traces (turn about and all that!) of a truly poetic sensibility in your work. You are obviously intelligent, well-read, sensitive, etc.

But it seems to me (and I cannot stress too strongly that this is a purely personal opinion—in fact, not even an opinion so much as a gut feeling, if you will) that you would do better in the medium of prose. I think the broader scope of a novel, or even a short story, would help you to develop your personae and your extremely interesting ideas. This is something one of my creative writing teachers told me once, and I've always been grateful to him for his honesty.

If you want to continue with the poetry, of course, that's your prerogative. If you do decide to stick with it, though, then my advice would be to choose something other than death to write about. Of all the subjects about which to write poetry, it seems to me, death is apt to produce the worst writing. If you want my honest opinion, I don't think anybody's been able to come up with even a half-way decent poem about the thing, including Donne and Thomas and whomever else you wish to include. Frankly, I look at it this way—death is just something that happens. We make a big deal out of it because it terrifies the hell out of us; when one looks at it objectively, though, one finds it is a good subject for a writer (particularly a poet) to steer away from.

As a matter of fact, I can't think of a more boring topic—unless it's daffodils!

Looking forward to hearing from you, I remain

Sincerely yours,
Prof. "Casey" Jedenacht

Dear Prof. Jedenacht:

As you will see from the enclosed, I took your advice about trying to express myself (much as I hate that phrase) in prose. I tried to take your other major piece of advice and write about something relatively positive, but the latter attempt, as you will soon discover, utterly failed. I find myself unable to write about anything except death.

And yet, I am not completely without hope that "Lucite" will strike some small spark of interest in you: after all, the persona's attitude toward the thing is very largely the same as I take yours to be.

Very truly yours,
Evelyn

Lucite

My father died when I was thirteen years old. I remember because that was my year for Lucite.

Perhaps a little background information would be of use here before I proceed.

I am—and if I am, I undoubtedly always was—a genius. I am also extremely wealthy. I am also what I suppose you would call "a cold fish"; as far as I'm concerned, that's the only rational way to be.

Oh, I know most people believe in love and friendship and emotions and all that; in fact, one of my earliest maxims was "The worse something is, the more people tend to believe in it." I don't want to get into a discussion of Nazism or anything like that, not at this point. You want to hear about my father's death and I'm here to oblige you. About the love business, though: the two kinds of love which are most universally acclaimed are the parental-filial and the amorati. Allow me simply to point out that modern psychologists agree with me that the first is no more or less than a dependency bond. (As a person who could have survived by his own wits from an early age, I never really, or at least consciously, knew what it was to feel dependent.) As for romantic love, I shall exercise my well-known classical restraint and limit myself to pointing out that the concept of romantic love qua concept was invented as late as the thirteenth century by troubadours and minnesingers who probably dreamed it up as what we today would call "a promotion gimmick."

So much for love.

Now I know a lot of you are probably "feeling sorry" for me, and I can assure you there is no need. Perhaps you would not wish to grant me the right to use the term "happy." So be it. But I consider that my life is "blest," as a character in Joseph Andrews expressed it, since I continually "experience the falsehood of common assertions." When my father died, I did not have any feelings of guilt or sadness. I hardly knew my father—as, indeed, I hardly knew, or know, anyone. He seemed pleasant enough, you understand, and I was glad (as opposed to grateful) not to have been born to a cruel or a stupid man. But that was all.

When mother came into my room, I was at work making a pair of Lucite bookends. As most of my biographers have pointed out, my fame as an innovator in the field of crafts could have been predicted almost from the very beginning by anyone with a modicum of intelligence and sensitivity. Fortunately or unfortunately, I myself was the only such person then acquainted with my work. I was always careful not to do too well in school, of course, since I knew all too well the resentment that would have stirred up in my peers and the annoying consequences I would have had to put up with.

Still, however, despite all my precautions on this score, I encountered a certain amount of residual hostility among my fellow students, particularly the boys.

It was partly in order to minimize this residual antipathy that I first began doing work with Lucite. One boy of rather pronounced sadistic tendencies asked me to build him "a home for my guinea pig." The resulting cage was quite satisfactory. I built a number of cages for the pets (I privately referred to them as "the nameless horrors") of the other boys.

Then I began making book-ends. On the night my father died, I had just finished the well-known "Black-and-White Pony Book Ends" which I understand are the earliest pieces featured in the Smithsonian. It was the first time I had ever really carved the Lucite, and the first time I had ever used a pictorial motif.

Anyway, when my mother told me my father had died—this may shock some of you—I was rather pleased. I had read all kinds of stories about children being made to kiss the lipsticked mouths of departed relatives and so on, and I suppose I hoped for something of the sort—anything, really, that would relieve the tedium of life in general.

Of course, nothing of the sort occurred. My father's casket was closed and the entire funeral service carried out in a quiet, dignified, and hence boring manner. To be sure, my mother cried a bit, but I had seen her cry as much when her mother's porcelain vegetable dish broke.

As it turned out, my father had left instructions that he be cremated: again, I had some expectations of drama—the casket sliding precipitously down into the roaring flames, and so on. Again, I was cheated. In fact, the family, at my mother's request, was not even present when the cremation took place.

A messenger brought us father's remains the following day. Mother didn't know what to do with them, she said, since father had left no instructions as to their disposal. She didn't want them walled up in some columbarium, with the other "cinery urns," she asserted. Nor did she "want the thing cluttering up the house and making people uncomfortable." I said I would be glad to keep the urn (it looked like a coffee can, I thought, for all that it had "R.I.P."

engraved on the top). With only the slightest of hesitations, she agreed.

I think the rest is pretty well-known to you all. It took me only a few days to hit upon the idea of sifting the remains to get out the bone fragments and embedding a handful of the finest ash in a book-end. From there, it was only a small step to the whole line of "Loved Ones in Lucite" which first brought me fame and fortune.

Dear Evelyn,

To begin with, I'm delighted that you took my advice about trying out the short story form. I definitely feel that you're on the right track, although perhaps not quite yet at the station! *Calcite* seems to me very good for a first attempt. In fact, for a piece of its kind I think it's truly excellent; the only problem is, I think what you've written is not so much a story as it is a character portrait—the kind of thing Browning might have written if he'd written prose.

The main ingredient of a story is action, it seems to me, and not point-of-view, although, of course, point-of-view can be very important. What I'd suggest is that you try, in your next story, to develop a sequence of events—try to weave a narrative thread, as it were.

Also, if you must write about death, perhaps you could approach it from a more positive—at least a less morbid or offbeat—angle. If you could choose a more normal persona, I think you would appeal to a wider audience.

Keep up the good work.

Very truly yours,
Prof. K.C. Jedenacht

Dear Sir:

As usual, I agreed with the criticisms you made in your letter. Enclosed please find my latest attempt to please you.

Sincerely yours,
evelyn trace

Catharsis

For purely personal reasons, I want to describe what she was like and how it happened.

She was so beautiful it almost hurt to look at her. She was very small and delicate, with skin so fair it seemed translucent. She had thick, dark hair that kind of swirled around, framing her little locket-face. I guess it was her high cheekbones and rather deep-set eyes that gave her a pathetically proud expression; she looked like a little girl facing her First Confession—not that that explains anything.

I suppose in her own way she was intelligent, but she got good grades mainly by virtue of her photographic memory. Being the kind of person who'd forget his head if it weren't attached, I really envied her that memory.

"God, school would be so much easier to take if I could only remember everything, like you do," I commented once.

"It's not that I can remember," she said. "It's just that I can't forget."

Not only did she remember everything she read, heard or saw, however—unfortunately, she also tended to believe it. This uncritical acceptance of things prevented her from doing any real scholarship. Her papers always represented impressive but ultimately unsuccessful attempts to reconcile incompatible views.

Her term paper on Chamberlain was a perfect case in point. After skimming through it, I took her to task. "First, you side with those who think he was a schmuck, then you agree with the 'unsung hero' faction," I said. "Don't give me that 'hobgoblin of little minds' business, either. Just accept the fact that you can't have things both ways."

She mumbled something about black-and-white ponies and about light's being both a particle and a wave; I didn't pay too much attention. After a few minutes, she smiled ruefully and said: "Well, I've heard that most student papers tend to throw out the baby with the bath. At least I don't do that—I just try to diaper the water."

Naturally, her penchant for accepting things at face value stood her in good stead socially. She came as close to being a real aristocrat as any Midwestern

Catholic can, but she never had that air of inaccessibility most people of her class exhibit. Average people felt at home with her.

There were widespread rumors to the effect that she was a little too accessible, particularly when it came to men, but when I heard things like that, I just shrugged them off. For one thing, she was pretty religious. More importantly, though, it was hard for me to imagine anyone's being promiscuous who was as uninterested in sex as she was. I say uninterested because although she never put me off or turned me down, not even during her periods, she never initiated anything either.

Unfortunately, her doctor had advised her not to take the pill. (Something to do with her having inherited a tendency to develop embolisms—it seems they can prove fatal if they travel to the heart—which meant birth control pills were dangerous for her.) Anyway, what with her passivity and my having to wear a condom, sex wasn't all that satisfactory....

It sounds funny, I guess, but the best times we had were spent in discussing rather sad and serious things. I had her read my thesis on the Aristotelian aspects of Euripides, since she had read most of his plays. Although she had read them while quite young, she remembered everything in them and more.... She started talking about Medea's having cooked her children and served them up to their father, for example; I'm afraid I teased her unmercifully about that.

On the lighter side, she liked my collection of famous last words ("Puto deus fio") and treasured phrases from children's nursery rhymes. Her favorite, which she claimed had something to do with a battle, was typical of the kind of thing she liked. It started innocently enough with reference to a garden full of seeds (weeds?). But it went on to talk about a lion at the door and ended by saying, "When your heart begins to bleed/ You're dead, and dead, and dead, indeed."

She told me once her father used to feed her lines of gallows humor ("Why is dying like going to the bathroom?"—"When you gotta go, you gotta go") while she drank her warm milk at bedtime. With a father like that, I suppose it's no wonder she had a morbid streak. For a time, in high school, she wanted to be a poet: she wrote hundreds of strange little poems, all of them morbid:

Death moves toward me. I'm dancing—He cuts in
The gay young blade—I'm now at his disposal.
I get the point of Women's Lib,
Accept his generous proposal.

I don't really think I can tell you much more about her. I'll just try to describe what happened as near as I can recall it. I remember I had trouble unlocking the door. (I'd had a key made for myself. I'm not sure whether she really liked that or not, but she spent a lot of time in bed, the covers pulled up over her head, and I was afraid one time she wouldn't hear the buzzer.) I was carrying a pizza in one hand, a 6-pack in the other. I kicked the door shut behind me, turned off the TV., and set out plates and napkins. I don't remember what was said, except that she called me "Ivan" (after her literary hero, Ivan Karamazov), which was usually a good sign.

I poured the beer too quickly and some of it foamed over on to the rug. I started dabbing at the wet spots with my napkin but she told me her mother, who had bought the rug for her, had said it was "'a good rug and good rugs don't show stains.'" So I stopped dabbing.

After a while, I realized she wasn't eating. Usually, she ate whatever I put in front of her. I asked her about it, and she said she didn't want any more.

"How can you not want more when you haven't had any?" I wanted to know. She mumbled something about being a hunger artist, but bowed her head dutifully and began to eat.

She had told me a few weeks before that there was to be an important lecture-and-slide presentation on the Normandy invasion that evening, and I asked her what time it was supposed to start.

"8:00," she said. "But I don't think I'll go."

I was unpleasantly surprised: as far as I knew, she had never missed a single class or class-related event and now didn't seem the time to start.

"Why not?"

"I'm sick of having to brown-nose. Sick of educational insemination. Sick of being fed on the blood of gods. Sick of conceptual consumption, for Christ's sake!"

She rattled out the "k" sounds in a sort of rapid-fire machine gun stutter and it struck me that I had never seen her show any sign of temper before.

In a way, I was encouraged. I had held off making love to her for a couple of weeks, hoping for once she'd be the one to make the overtures. I don't know—I suppose I connected temper with passion somehow. I'd had several beers by then, and the weeks of abstinence had left me sort of sexed-up.

At any rate, I remember thinking maybe she wanted to stay home so we could have a real night of it. I guess that was when I asked her if she'd been to confession. (The next day was the Feast of the Epiphany, a holy day of obligation.)

She said no, she hadn't, adding that she didn't want to take communion any more. Again, I asked her why. She said something about swallowing's being for the birds and gagging's not being a joke. I really didn't pay much attention; the fact she wasn't planning to take communion sort of cinched things in my mind. I'm not sure what I said or did next. I do remember carrying her to bed and making rather short work of the situation.

I must have fallen asleep right away, because I woke up about an hour later and I was still on top of her and still attached, so to speak. She was wide-awake, apparently had been the whole time. Her eyes had a funny kind of glazed look. Her fists were clenched. Her whole body was rigid.

Needless to say, I immediately withdrew....

I vaguely remember making a few comments about the way she'd been acting the last couple of weeks. I finished by saying something like, "I don't know what's gotten into you lately."

She didn't say anything for a few minutes. Then she asked me where I bought the "Trojans" I kept in her bathroom cabinet. I told her and she nodded. "I thought so," she said.

Naturally, I didn't let it go at that. I kept after her until she revealed the following facts:

1) The pharmacy where I bought condoms had recently fired one of their employees;
2) The guy they fired was mentally ill; among other things, he amused himself by opening packages of condoms and making pin-prick holes in some of the tips;
3) She thought I must have purchased a batch which included some of these "punctured prophylactics;"
4) She had missed her last period and although the rabbit-test "hadn't taken" (and was thus inconclusive), she was pretty sure she was pregnant;
5) That's what had 'gotten into her' lately.

I was pretty upset by what she'd said, mostly because it made our whole relationship sound like something out of daytime TV. But I told myself it was no good sitting around thinking about what if she were pregnant, there would be time enough in the days ahead to decide what to do, and if she weren't, so much the better. It occurred to me that getting out and going to the lecture might be just the ticket in getting our minds off things. "At any rate, it can't hurt," I thought.

It was sleeting out, apparently had been for some time; ice had glassed over large stretches of the sidewalks. The winds seemed to be of gale force—"things too fierce to mention." I was wearing boots and a hooded parka, though, so I didn't mind too much.

We were a little late. The elevator didn't seem to be in operation so we went up the fire-stairs. I guess others had been that way before us; in any event, the fire-door had been propped open.

As we walked down the corridor, I noticed that all the office doors were shut and the air in the corridor was unusually close. I thought of going back and opening the window at the far end of the hall, but decided there wasn't time.

We got to the office where the talk was being given, and she opened the door.

Out of nowhere, there was an ear-splitting explosion. Dagger-like shards of glass flew past her and into the hall. Someone began to scream.

Instinctively, I pulled her back into the corridor. She was dry-eyed, but making strangled, mewing sounds; she seemed to be having some sort of convulsions.

Someone later tried to explain to me just what had happened. It seems the fire door's being the only thing open had set up a kind of air-trap. I don't know—the explanation was too scientific to mean very much to me. What I do know is that at the instant she opened the door to the lecture-room, the window imploded. (I also learned later that, despite the screaming, no one had been seriously hurt.)

Well, all I could think of then was that I had to get her out of there. Whatever had happened in the room was not her fault and nothing whatever would be achieved by our hanging around. Besides, she was obviously in a state of shock.

I led her back to the apartment. When we arrived, I got her to drink some warm milk while I finished the 6-pack. I gave her a tentative kiss, but there was a noticeable lack of response, so I turned in, advising her to do the same. ("Sleep knits up the raveled sleeve of care" and all that.)

As I recall, she said she'd "be right there."

When I woke up the next morning, she wasn't in bed; one look at her pillow (in her sleep, she really mauled the thing) told me she hadn't been there at all.

I was heading for the study when I saw the note adhesive-taped to the bathroom door. In her curious, backhand scrawl, she had written: "I would be afraid of a less expressive death."

It's impossible to lock that door, but somehow she had managed to jam it shut. I forced it open, and peered in.

It was the most awful thing I've ever seen. (Luckily, I've pretty much managed to blot the sight out of my mind.) She had gotten into the bath tub—it was full—and cut her throat. There was blood everywhere....

Being somewhat of a classicist, I don't think tragedies can be explained; I think they're to be felt rather than understood.... Describing what happened, reliving the pity and terror of it all, hasn't been easy, but I feel better for having done so. Things have a way of working out.

Dear Evelyn,

Now you're really getting it together, as some of my other students like to say. I liked your story very much. I think this time you chose the right point-of-view and the subject is pretty much within the parameters of popular tastes. (What could be more normal than a guy getting his girl pregnant, right?)

The tissue of references and symbolic actions (spilling beer on the rug and all that) seems carefully, though perhaps a trifle too obtrusively (with an "r"!), elaborated. I haven't really had time to think about whether Euripides and the Latin ("I think I am making a god") and so on are truly inevitable in the story, but they sound good just on the surface of it, and I'm willing to take your word for the rest.

The only case which strikes me as a possible exception to the above is the girl's reference to a pony of some sort. Now I noticed horse references in a couple of your other things if I remember right, and I had trouble with the darn things then, too.... Probably ponies and horses and the like serve as some kind of private symbol for you—that's fine. But when you're writing a story, you have to make all your references at least potentially accessible to the reader. Not only that, but in this particular case, your private way of looking at horses—which I take to be almost completely asexual—directly conflicts with the standard (Freudian, neo-Freudian, psychoanalytic, whatever) way of looking at them. I suggest that you leave this particular warhorse (my puns are deliberate, too!) to the authorities and choose something else to be private about!

Enough of the harangue, already! Just one more point: although I think *Catharsis* is far and away the best thing you've written, it—like your other pieces—takes much too long to get going. Your beginning is more or less just deadwood, just straight exposition. I would suggest that the next time you do as Hemingway used to do: write your story, then go back and cut the first paragraph or two. (He used to cut the endings off as well, I believe, but I think your work is quite all right in that department.)

Incidentally, may I take this opportunity to remind you that additional coursework, according to the terms of that ad you liked so much, necessitates another financial remission on your part. How time does fly, eh?

Well, with that word to the wise, I remain

Yours truly,
"Casey" Jedenacht

Dear Sir:

Enclosed please find my latest and last submission. I am aware that it is not strictly covered by the terms of our agreement; I sent it to you as a kind of "thank you," in the hope you will find it enjoyable—or at least edifying.

Happy criticizing!
evelyn trace
N.B. I am a woman.

Famous Last Words

She had not wanted a lingering death; she had wanted to "go out like a light," as her husband, a well-known journalist, had put it. That was how he had gone—a stroke in his sleep.

But turning misfortunes into their opposite had always been her strong point. This lingering death (her death), seen positively, represented a chance to get even, somehow. (With whom, for what, she didn't know.)

"Life imitates art," her husband had been fond of saying. She was experiencing the truth of that now.

As a girl, millennia ago, she had wanted to be a writer. She had written a story called "Famous Last Words" about an unbelievably old woman, lying on her deathbed, who was determined to go out with a flourish, if not a bang.

Now she herself was unbelievably old.... If she could just remember the story and follow it, she would be acting the lead in her own play. She could die in the service of her own creation. She could be the artist of her own destruction.

The trouble was, she couldn't remember how the story ended.... She remembered that her first thought had been to have the old woman choke to death in the middle of a tantalizing sentence: "The only thing that really matters is—" But even in her youth, she had had enough sense to reject that idea. "Dime-novel stuff," her husband would have called it.

Another possibility she'd considered was that of having the old woman be successful—say just what she wanted to say—and then die happy. The problem with that approach, apart from the fact that most people nowadays didn't believe one could 'die happy', was that it wasn't playing fair with the public not to tell them what those last words were. And if one elected to play it straight, what words could one put in the story-woman's mouth that would be meaningful but mysterious, etc., that would justify all the narrative build-up?

Of course, one could play the thing for laughs: have the old woman come out with a kind of vaudeville routine—"I'm goin' fast, but 'afore I go, I got one thing to say: 'I'm goin' fast.'" But she had rejected that idea, too. It was too much like masturbating: (Her husband had said masturbation was "carried out in frustration, and concluded in defeat." "Even when it's good, it's bad," he had remarked.)

She had considered other endings and rejected them in turn: having the old bat's "famous last words" turn out to be gibberish ("The moon is an eagle") or something somebody else had already said ("More light") or a variation on it ("Less light," even "More life"), but all those endings were cheap, they were cop-outs, and she had never been one in favor of copping out.

A more attractive possibility had been having the old woman do something (give her grand-daughter a rose or a shiny new quarter) rather than trying to speak. But a story like that wouldn't be much more than a moralistic cliché (Her husband had called such pronouncements "profundisms"), like "Life must go on" or even (God forbid) "Actions speak louder than words."

She had also considered an epilogue-ending: the old woman would say something personally meaningful (like "Rosebud"), then there would be a significant space, then a sentence like "The doctor put away his stethoscope and, turning to the husband (son? father?), said: 'You can be thankful it was a stroke—she never knew what hit her.'"

All those endings and others had been rejected: she remembered that. But she couldn't remember, she simply could not remember, how she had ended the story. Maybe she hadn't finished it at all, in fact; maybe that was it.

Even if it had never been finished, though, she knew it had been a good story. Thinking too much about endings, after all, was a mistake: you have an idea; you write a story. The story ends whenever you stop writing.

Dear Evelyn:

Famous Lost Words was excellent. I'm only sorry you chose not to go on with me. As one of my sidelines, I publish a small journal. With a little polishing, your story might well have proved suitable for publication.

If you should change your mind, you know where I am! Until then, I remain,

Very truly yours,
Kathy Christine Jedenacht

ON THE TOPMOST BRANCH
OF A BECKETT TREE

Minutes into their first date, she knew. There was passion in him, but muted. Buried, as if in a vault. Underwater. Not dangerous at all. Comforting, even. No explosion would send emotional tsunamis racing for shore. What there was would just warm the environment slightly. Like an electric blanket. One that could be adjusted, but not beyond demarcated limits. He was perfect.

When he saw her, something in him rose like an eagle on a high updraft of possibility. He wanted to dive. He wanted to swoop down and carry her off. He was newly strong and forceful and could afford to be a little demanding. She might protest at the beginning, but soon she would enjoy it all—his demand, her protest, the eventual subsuming of separateness in one barbaric yawp.

The pinch-faced waitress vanished after mumbling reassurances, and he started talking. The things he said were standard first date fare—What about this weather? Have you been here before? But he had gotten hold of a fork somewhere, and he made little stroking motions with it. He pawed at the napkin, the place mat, sometimes the table— fingernails on a blackboard. Was it too soon, five minutes in, to ask him please to stop?

She didn't have much to say. She nodded a lot, even when he hadn't said anything. As though she understood everything. What he said and what he didn't say. As though she already knew and trusted him and was giving him permission to set the tone, to set the stage, to set the great enterprise in motion. She never looked at him for long. Everything about her was delicate.

He went from the weather to divorce and then to sex before the knock-kneed waitress had even had the good sense to return. He didn't call it sex, though. He called it intimacy. He called it love-making. He paused before each synonym and his eyes flared. Why didn't he just say the word, and be done with it? He leaned farther and farther forward. Where were his legs under the table? His hands had disappeared. Where was that waitress?

Now she wasn't even glancing at him. She cast her gaze demurely at the table. Her ivory face was like a little locket. The scarf was loosely fastened around her neck. How? There was no sign of a clip or a knot. If he pulled on the long end, what would happen? It was silk, for sure. Ruby and russet. She had missed a button on her blouse. It folded softly there, inviting closer inspection. This small detail seemed a private message to him. Not a text. A telegram on yellow paper: *Thinking of meeting you, my fingers fumbled. Stop. I look down now lest I should seem too bold. Stop.*

He began to ask sexual questions, though he still clung to synonyms. Clearly, he was taking liberties. Maybe this was another walk out situation. But he didn't seem to expect answers and his tone was unassuming, affectionate, somehow. He spoke in awkward word-clusters—clusters that trailed off, stepped into an elevator, but didn't push any button. *When your ex came on to checkout girls, did you ever wonder...? The last time you were intimate, did you realize...?*

She was flushed now and her breathing became a little wispy, a trifle erratic. Every once in a while, she would glance at him with her soulful eyes, and he wanted to take her silky clothes off and kiss her everywhere. But there was more than the promise of sex here. More and deeper and amazingly, there was love. He loved her. He had managed it finally—he had fallen in love right away, at first sight. He would give her the gift of time—time to adjust, to comply. He would not ruin it with urgency.

She didn't know where to look. Where in Christ's name was that snarky little waitress? His eyes had gone saucery. His mouth hung slightly open. Was he one of those who saw women as pastries to be gobbled up? Had he forgotten where they were? The coffee shop was called Intimate Encounters, but there was nothing to substantiate the title, just chrome and vinyl. Her silence only seemed to encourage him. Was it too late to ask him where he worked, return things to the level plains of statistics?

She needed reassurance. He reached out under the table. The eagle flew low across a chasm, a yawning abyss, and came gently, gently to rest. Spread thumb and fingers told him he had landed on her knee. Her left knee. The fingertips touched what had to be her skirt. Silk again. He could almost hear the rustle. But his palm was resting lightly on flesh. Vulnerable, silken flesh, and under that, vulnerable white bone. If he could find the words...express love with sound as well as touch. There was a taste in the air like salt. The colorful boardwalks of his childhood beckoned, endless and epheme—

The eagle was pushed off its perch and plummeted. "What do you think you're doing?"

"I just wanted to—"

"You fucking men are all alike."

"No, I think it's the reverse of what Tolstoy said about families. Unhappy unfucking men are all alike, whereas happily fucking men.... Wait. You're upset. Was it the knee pat? I wasn't coming on to you. I was just trying to reassure you."

"*You* were trying to reassure *me?* That's perfect." She sneered, she stood, she stalked out.

The waitress overturned a cup and poured coffee without his asking, as though he were already a regular. "First date?"

"Yeah. First of no more. I really thought this was different. I still managed to ruin it somehow."

"I've been there, believe me."

The coffee smelled good, and the waitress's smile was like warm honey sliding over breakfast toast.

On the topmost branch of a Beckett tree, the eagle landed.